A Cowboy for April

A Cowboy for April

A Three Sisters Ranch Romance

Jamie K. Schmidt

TULE
PUBLISHING

Chapter One

A PRIL GRAYSON CLENCHED her jaw and tried not to cry as she removed her personal stuff from the desk she had busted her ass at for the last five years.

Downsized.

Carefully, she put the picture frames of her sisters' rodeo championships in the copier paper box the security guard had handed to her. He was busy watching the other four people who had gotten the axe during the morning meeting as they also packed up their things.

She wasn't sure what she was going to do now. She was still numb. Her fingers shook as she took down the map of Europe. April had marked all the places where she wanted to go with a smiley-face pin. Panic flared again before she could keep a lid on it. She had carefully planned out a European cruise and she'd almost had enough money to pay for it. Now, unless she tapped into that fund, she'd be lucky to afford the next three months in her studio apartment in downtown Austin. It wasn't fair. She'd waited all her life to see the world instead of four cubicle walls and a computer screen. Maybe she could find another job quickly.

April didn't like maybes. She liked absolutes.

Her cell phone rang. It was her mother. Oh hell, not now. But when it stopped ringing and immediately started up again, she locked eyes with the security guard.

"I've got to take this."

He gave her a sympathetic nod. He knew she wasn't the type of person to cause trouble. In fact, he had often let her into the building on weekends and signed her out late at night after everyone had gone home. She was the last person who should have been let go. But tell that to the corporate overlords.

"Yeah," she said huskily into the phone.

"I know you're working, baby doll. I won't keep you long. I just want to know if you're coming home this weekend."

"I hadn't planned on it." Home had been a double wide in the Hickory Creek trailer park in Last Stand, until April had gone off to college and her sisters went off on the circuit. While her sisters had made a name for themselves being professional barrel racers, April had busted her butt getting her certificate of public accounting.

"I need you to come home right away."

April closed her eyes. What now? If it wasn't one emergency, it was another. Her two sisters were out on the rodeo circuit all over the United States. Not that they'd be a damn bit of help if her mother's current crisis was financial—which it usually was. They spent money like it was a renewable resource and for them, for a very short window of time, it was. April didn't begrudge her sisters their fun. They worked hard. They trained hard, and they put everything out there for their fans and for their love of the sport. But April was tired of being the sensible one. And she was tired of being the responsible one.

April had worked hard through college and all the way up to getting her CPA, much to her sisters' and her mother's amusement. Their eyes crossed whenever the talk of budgeting, money, or anything math-related came up. Her mother was a rodeo queen. Her sisters were rodeo queens. April was an accountant. That pretty much summed up her family dynamics.

"What's wrong?" April had to force lightness that she didn't feel into her voice, otherwise her mother might burst into tears and it would take longer to get the story out of her. Not for the first time, she felt like she was the mother instead of the middle child.

"He took everything," her mother sobbed.

April pulled back her wheeled chair and sat down. This was going to be a long one. To satisfy the security guard, April tucked her phone between her cheek and shoulder and continued to empty the desk drawer of ramen noodle cups and bagged tuna fish packages.

"Johnny Ray?" April asked.

"No," her mother scoffed. "I broke it off with Johnny Ray three months ago."

"I can't keep up," she murmured. Mama went through men like they were jelly beans. Unfortunately, the ones she chose weren't watermelon-flavored. They were like the prank jelly beans that tasted like vomit and ear wax.

"This was Stuart."

Stuart was new. April usually heard about the boyfriends once the new car smell of them wore off. "What happened? Did he need money for his mother's surgery? Or was it a once-in-a-lifetime investment?" April had heard this all before. Her mother never learned.

"He said he needed five hundred dollars to get his car back on the road. He had a job interview and he needed to pay the garage cash so they would fix it fast. He was going to pay me back as soon as he landed the job. But I haven't heard from him in three days."

"Uh-huh." April threw out a squishy stress ball with Austin Accounting firm on it. The bright side to all this is she wouldn't need that anymore. Now she'd have new stresses to worry about. "So all he got was five hundred dollars?"

"Yes," her mother wailed. "It was my last five hundred dollars."

That wasn't exactly true. April had set her mother and her two sisters up with bank accounts that only April could access. Of course, they had their own checking accounts, but there was rarely more than a thousand dollars in them at any one time. A long time ago, the four of them agreed to direct deposit their paychecks into the accounts that April controlled. Otherwise, the money would be gone as fast as they earned it. A percentage of their paychecks went into their personal checking accounts, but most of their money went to pay their bills and into savings. Sometimes April felt like a control freak, but this process had kept phone calls like this to a minimum.

"How much do you need?" April would send her the

money once her mother promised to go back to direct deposit.

"I need a thousand dollars."

"What?" April barked.

The security guard frowned at her. She resisted the urge to give him the finger.

"For household things," her mother said shakily.

"Bullshit."

Another frown from the security guard.

April had set it up that all her mother's bills got paid automatically out of the locked-down account. A spare thought hit her, though.

"Did you get another credit card?" With her mother's credit, that should have been impossible, but there was always a predatory company around that was willing to loan money to someone who was down on their luck—with an exorbitant interest rate.

Her mother sighed. "You're going to be mad at me."

Oh, this wasn't good.

"I've been having Stella pay me in cash instead of direct depositing my check into that Fort Knox account."

April's computer access had been taken away. Otherwise, she'd be logging into that account now to see the damage. She didn't dare try to do that on her phone while she was talking with her mother. The security guard giving her the stink eye as it was. April needed to hurry up and vacate the premises before they escorted her out. "I thought we agreed that you'd keep your tips for mad money and deposit your salary," she said in a fast whisper.

Her mother worked as a hair stylist at the local salon. She had been one of the most glamorous rodeo queens in Last Stand and had a loyal clientele that loved how she transformed them with some of that star quality she still had. Her mother was magic with a curling iron and a pair of scissors.

"We did. And I know you're right. But I didn't want to wait until I saved up enough money to buy a few new dresses. Stuart liked to go out to fancy places."

"Let me guess. You paid." To heck with this. Austin Accounting could throw the rest of this crap out. April had to get out of here. She had her pictures and her favorite coffee mug. The less stuff she had to carry, the better.

"Well, it was just until he got this new job."

"So what's the thousand dollars for?" Shrugging into her coat, April placed her purse in the copier box, making sure not to scratch up the pictures of her cat Cheddar, and of Merry and June on their horses at the Women's Rodeo World Championship last year.

"Mr. Jonas," her mother said with a defeated sigh. "I've been sweet-talking him for a while now. But he's going to kick me and Tulip out if I don't pay him by tomorrow morning."

Tulip was her mother's pony from hell. He was a nippy little tyrant and April wouldn't mind seeing him homeless. Unfortunately, he and her mother were a package deal. Still, April hadn't been planning on making the drive to Last Stand tonight, even if her life hadn't been turned upside down.

"Are you still there?" her mother said nervously.

"Yeah, sorry. I had to finish up something. I've got to go. I'll call you right back."

"But..."

She hung up on her mother and slid the phone into her jacket pocket. Thrusting her copier box at the security guard, she tapped her foot impatiently while he made sure she wasn't stealing office supplies. There was one good thing to all of this: April no longer felt like crying and she was mad enough at her mother that she took it out by glaring at all the managers on her way out.

Unfortunately, she lost her bravado on the way down to the parking garage. What the hell was she going to do? She had a thousand dollars in her own savings to cover her mother. But that wasn't what she was worried about.

No, she was worried about paying her own rent and finding another job in this economy. A part of her wanted to go to Last Stand this weekend and stay there. April was sick of the city anyway, with the overpriced rent, overpriced food, overpriced everything. And she wasn't ready to get another job where she was just a corporate drone in a soulless company. But what was the alternative?

Then suddenly, it hit her. She could go out on her own. After all, she was a CPA and tax season was coming up.

April broke out in a cold sweat. Start her own business? She'd have to do a cost analysis. Weigh the pros and cons. This wasn't something she could do on an impulse. Hell, she couldn't do anything without overthinking it. Her family had lived their entire lives by the creed, "What have you got to lose?" but April wasn't wired that way. April had spent her whole life making sure she had a plan, and everyone stuck to it or there would be hell to pay. She followed all the rules because her mother and sisters didn't think rules applied to them and April had seen firsthand how well that had turned out. So instead, she played it safe, going into accounting after high school. There were no gray areas in numbers. Numbers didn't lie. They always followed rules and they were easy to predict. Her sisters went on to build their rodeo careers up until they were big stars. They partied hard and dated sexy cowboys and lived for fun and excitement.

Excitement for April was ordering Chinese food mid-week.

She shook her head, disappointed in herself. Look where being safe and secure had gotten her. Her sisters were having the time of their lives doing what they loved, and she'd just been let go from a job she'd almost got an ulcer for. Now the clock had already started counting down—she'd soon be homeless as well as jobless. She wondered how her sisters would react when she told them that Austin Accounting had thrown a grenade in the middle of her ten-year plan.

June would laugh and then drag April out to get drunk. After all, if something didn't work out for June, she always seemed to find another opportunity right around the corner. As the baby of the family, June considered the song "Don't Worry, Be Happy" as her personal anthem.

It should have been annoying, but June always knew how to cheer her up and put a positive spin on everything. Of course, she also had the most outrageous ideas and would run headlong into schemes without thinking them through.

While April's head would practically explode thinking of all the ways things could go wrong, her sister just shrugged off consequences. In fact, April felt a little bit of that panic creeping up her throat right now.

Merry, on the other hand, would have to be restrained from storming into Austin Accounting and kicking someone's ass. Anyone's ass. Merry took her role as big sister to heart. She was the family's avenging angel—even when they didn't need to be avenged. Everyone knew to stay out of Merry's way when she was on a tear. She could be a gold-star diva when she wanted to be, but if she liked you, you'd never doubt that she was in your corner.

April should call them, but it was the middle of the day and they were probably in the barn or with their horses. Besides, she should probably come clean and tell her mother first. She needed to understand that April was in a difficult place.

Her mother would be terrified when she found out that April had lost her job. April was her rock. The person she could go to for a thousand-dollar loan because she knew April would have it in her savings. But April was terrified too. Her savings was about to be plundered like a pirate chest in the Caribbean.

It seemed like forever, but she finally made it through the walk of shame and was standing by her car. She shoved her box into the passenger seat, and then got in the car. She just stared out the windshield, trying to take it all in. April had made a vow a long time ago that she would never allow herself to be at the whims of fate. This wasn't her role in life.

She was the quiet one, the reliable one. The one who everyone went to when their lives fell apart.

Sure, she was twenty-seven years old and this was the first time the shit had hit the fan for her. That wasn't so bad, right?

It wasn't…except there was no one she could turn to for help.

Her phone rang again.

"Here we go." April put the car into gear and had the call go through the car's speaker system so she could talk hands-free.

"I need you to bring him the cash," her mother said as if there hadn't been a break in their conversation. "Mr. Jonas is not going to trust a check. The bank has declined the recurring payment for the trailer park rental."

"Was it worth it, Mama?" April said, unable to keep the sigh out of her voice.

"While it was happening, yeah. Now, not so much. Maybe if you went a little wild once in a while, you'd know what it was like."

Yeah, right. Someone had to be the adult in this family. But she didn't say that. Her mother had been hurt enough. And if her mother hadn't learned by now that life wasn't about living in the moment, she wasn't going to.

"I can't come down this weekend." April had to draw a line in the sand somewhere.

"B-but…" Her mother's voice was high and panicked.

April took a deep breath. She had to get a word in edgewise. "I just got laid off from my job. I need the weekend to consider my options and I can't do that in Last Stand." It was like she had just ripped a bandage off a fresh wound. She felt raw and exposed.

Her mother's attitude switched from helpless maiden to avenging Valkyrie. "Yes, you can. You come home right now. You can stay here. I'll take care of you. I've got some hamburger in the freezer and I'm sure there's some wine around here somewhere."

April felt a smile tug on her lips. Her mother had a lot of faults, but she loved April and her sisters fiercely. "I need some time to process this all on my own. But thank you."

"I heard that Trent Campbell is looking for an accountant to help him with back taxes," she said.

"Where did you hear that?" Trent had married Kelly Sullivan last year and the two of them had built a house on her family's ranch. April and Kelly had been good friends in high school, but after Kelly had gotten pregnant and left Last Stand, they had grown apart. But they'd reconnected earlier this year when April had been in town, visiting her mom. Kelly was now six months pregnant and had morning, afternoon, and evening sickness. The only thing that helped her was ginger tea and shortbread cookies. There was a tearoom in Austin that carried both and April had been sending Kelly a stash every week. But her friend hadn't mentioned any tax problems when they'd chatted last week.

"He put up signs around town and a few people were talking about it in the salon. He wants to hire local. It's temporary, but at least it would be something."

"I'm not local," April said, getting into the slow lane so

the car crawling up on her could pass.

"Of course you are. You're a Grayson. We're famous in Last Stand."

Infamous was more like it. June had done a Lady Godiva down Main Street one summer to advertise a community theater production. Merry had chased off a bunch of city punks who had come into Last Stand to cause trouble by roping a few of them and bringing them to Police Chief Highwater. And Mama had stormed the announcers' table at the Last Stand Rodeo and demanded over the PA system that she'd "had enough of all these cowboys. Where the hell were the cow*men*?"

April snorted. "I'm not one of the wild Graysons."

"Of course you are. Or you could be, if you gave yourself the chance."

It was laughable, but at the same time a spark of longing hit her deep in her soul. What would it be like to just let go and let life happen organically?

"Last Stand is your home, April."

"I don't know, Mama." April put on her blinker. She definitely wouldn't miss the commute to downtown Austin every day.

"What have you got to lose?"

April's gut clenched. She had lost her job and was probably going to lose her apartment. If she could get ahead of things, though, she might still be able to realign her goals to her ten-year plan. "I'll give Kelly a call. I'll wire her the money and she can pay Mr. Jonas, but you've got to promise me that you'll ask Stella to go back to direct depositing your paycheck."

"I will," her mother said. "I promise. Come home as soon as you can."

"We'll see," April said, hanging up.

The way April saw it, she could curl up in a ball and lament that her carefully laid plans had been shredded, or she could pivot and use this as a way to reinvent herself. Did she like having everything planned down to the last minute?

No, but it was comforting in its own way.

But comfort was starting to feel like a prison.

How would her life have been different if June had been riding Ares that day? Was there an alternate universe out there where April Grayson was a rodeo star? Was she happy? Her mind flitted back through all her regrets.

She regretted choosing Ares because he was a gorgeous horse instead of looking at his temperament.

She regretted not kissing Cole Lockwood when he gave her a ride home from the rodeo.

She regretted not taking a year off to travel between high school and college. She had been too afraid to stay at the youth hostels. And too afraid to leave her mother and sisters alone.

Playing it safe hadn't saved her job. Fear had driven most of her life decisions. And she hadn't been able to escape it. Fear was in the backseat, waiting to jump into the driver's seat even now. But April couldn't let that happen. Not this time. And yet there had to be a way she could step out of her comfort zone without going crazy.

For once she was glad of the heavy traffic—it kept her

mind off all the ways things could go wrong if she threw caution to the wind and became what she'd always wanted to be—a wild Grayson sister.

Chapter Two

C OLE LOCKWOOD SHOULD have stayed home and caught up on sleep when his high-stakes poker game got canceled at the last minute. He had been working back-to-back jobs for the past three months, saving up for the buy-in.

When he hadn't been working, he had been helping to remodel his parents' home, so they didn't have to go up and down the stairs. Even when he had been out on the poker circuit, Cole knew he always had a place to come back to and he was determined that his parents would live out their lives in the comfort of their own house instead of a nursing home.

Their ranch that had been in his family for generations, dating back to the first Last Stand developments. Some days, it was too much house and land for them. But most of the time, Cole was proud of what generations of his family had done in the past to make Last Stand the thriving community it was today.

And so, if that meant that they had to rearrange the house so that all the bedrooms were on the ground floor and they had an accessible shower, bathroom, and laundry there, well, Cole was willing to put in the extra work to do that.

There wasn't a day that went by that he didn't kick himself for not being better with his money. If he'd even saved half of his poker winnings, he wouldn't have to work two jobs now.

But there had always been a trip with his buddies, or a new truck to buy. And the renovations on his parents' place hadn't come cheap, either, though he'd been more than happy to finance them if they made his parents' lives easier. Of course, that was back when he thought he was going to win a World Series of Poker bracelet. Like his rodeo career, his gambling venture hadn't panned out the way he'd planned either.

So yes, getting some sleep would have been the smart thing to do. A cold beer and some country music, however, was what he craved. And if he could find a pretty girl to dance with, that would soothe the frustration and disappointment at missing an opportunity to make some serious cash.

He decided to check out Buddy's Bar and Boogie in Whiskey River because they usually had live music on the weekends. Only tonight, instead of a band, they had a bunch of mechanical bulls set up as part of a beer promotion. He signed up to ride one, but only because there was a free beer in it. And he was pretty sure he could make a better showing than the one guy who got tossed, headfirst, over the fake horns.

While he waited his turn, he took in the crowd. There were some familiar faces. In line with him were even a few of the adult students who went to Trent Campbell's Rodeo

School. They exchanged nods. Cole mainly worked with the elementary and middle school kids, but he sometimes helped Trent and his father Billy with the adult classes when they needed an extra hand.

A brunette in a flashy dress caught his eye as she sashayed up to the bar. The red material clung in all the right places, so when she turned to look out at the bar, it was a few moments before his gaze reached her face.

A punch of recognition had him swallowing hard—April Grayson. He would have gone over to her, but the crowd was effectively blocking him in until after his ride. Cole would have to hope that the mechanical bulls would distract every randy cowboy in this place until he could get free. He looked his fill as she spoke with an older man who didn't seem to be hitting on her. Who would have thought that April Grayson would wear a dress like that?

She had been a few years behind him in high school, but she had been so damned smart, she had skipped ahead. Back then, they'd shared a few of the same classes, though she hadn't paid him a bit of attention, which was probably for the best. He hadn't wanted anything serious back then. He had been too busy with poker, rodeo and staying out all night long drinking beer and barely avoiding trouble.

But there had been that one time... Cole wondered if she remembered when he'd offered to drive her home from the Last Stand Rodeo. He'd been hoping she would invite him inside, but she had jumped out of his truck before he'd even put it into park. At the least, he'd been hoping for a kiss. But instead, all he'd gotten was just a breathy thank you, and then she was gone.

It was probably for the best. She'd had pretty eyes and a smile that made him think of pulling her into a corner somewhere. That hadn't changed. Her sisters had gone on to become big rodeo stars, but Cole had always wondered what happened to April. And now that she was back in town, he couldn't wait to find out.

"Hey, Cole!" A shout caught his attention.

Cole looked over and saw his friend Donovan Link in the crowd. He had his arm around his fiancée, Emily, but reached over the gated area to hand Cole a bottle of beer.

"Thank you," Cole said, taking a large swig.

"Don't you get enough of riding bulls during the work week?" Emily teased. She was Trent's sister-in-law and the manager of the Three Sisters Ranch, where Donovan had built a lodge that specialized in taking tourists on Texas safaris, as well as offering hunting trips that kept the feral hog problem in check.

"I'm just in it for the beer." He winced as a cowboy whirled around on the bull and landed on his chin on the inflatable mat.

"Have you thought about what we discussed earlier?" Donovan asked.

"No business." Emily elbowed him. "You promised to take me dancing. I want one night where we pretend the ranch will get by without us for a few hours."

"All right. All right." Donovan capitulated. "How are your parents?" he asked, changing the subject.

Cole would rather have talked business, which in this

case was the poker game that Donovan was trying to get him to host for his hunters. It wasn't really worth his time, but it would be fun. Unfortunately, right now, he had to concentrate on making money, not having fun.

"They're doing okay. Dad still thinks he's twenty-one and doesn't need his walker. Mom is in some residual pain, but she's moving around better. Every day I see an improvement." Cole shrugged. "It's just a matter of time."

"That's good to hear." Donovan clinked bottles with him.

The medical bills, on the other hand, were totally out of control. Cole had been counting on that now-canceled high-stakes game to finally get ahead of the bills. Instead, it looked like he was going to have to work days at Trent's as usual, and continue doing ranch jobs at night as they came up. He'd heard that Rick Braxton was down a ranch hand. Maybe Cole could pick up some hours at his place on the weekend.

"Hey, I think that's April Grayson over there. I'm going to say hi," Emily said, looking over at the bar.

"How do you know April?" Cole asked quickly, trying not to sound interested.

"We go way back. Her sister June and I used to raise hell during high school together." Emily waved, trying to get April's attention.

Cole almost swallowed his tongue when she looked over at them. It was like the noise in the bar faded away and he could only hear the strains of a Blake Shelton slow song.

She flushed red and her lips parted. Was he imagining

that she stared at him with hunger? Hell yeah, the night was looking up. He grinned at her.

"I'll go get her." Emily pushed her way through the crowd toward April.

"So, have you caught a game?" Donovan asked.

"Just online," Cole said disgustedly. "I had one lined up for tonight, but it fell through."

"That sucks."

More than Donovan knew.

"Hey, you're next," the promoter said.

"Shit." Cole tanked the rest of his beer and handed the bottle back to Donovan.

"Good luck." Donovan slapped him on the shoulder.

This would have been a lot easier if April hadn't been watching. He could feel her eyes on him as Emily dragged her back toward them. He looked over and winked at her. Yeah, that was definitely a blush. Now Cole could only hope he didn't make a gigantic ass out of himself. Bull riding wasn't his specialty. He had been a bulldogger. But considering he taught kids how to ride a mechanical bull, this could be embarrassing if he got tossed on his ass in eight seconds.

When it was his turn, he settled on top of the fake bull's wide back. He held on to the strap and raised his hand up. Luckily, after watching the first guy go ass over Stetson, he was prepared for the front lunge. Then, gripping the bull with his thighs, he settled in for the fast turn. And from there on in, it was a straight back and forth buck until the ride operator felt like being a dick and reversed directions.

Cole let himself fly off, knowing that the air mat would

cushion the blow. What he hadn't expected was to land perfectly in front of April Grayson. She stared down at him over the gate, her mouth open in surprise.

And like a true gambler, he looked up at her and asked, "Can I buy you a drink?"

Chapter Three

A PRIL STARED IN disbelief at the man she had been ogling for the past five minutes—the man now sprawled at her feet.

"Oh my gosh," she said. "You're Cole Lockwood." The man she had subconsciously compared every other man she had ever dated to. When she'd first caught sight of him across the bar, she hadn't realized she was looking at the real deal.

Cole blinked at her in surprise. "And you're April Grayson."

April tried not to appear flustered. He remembered her! Cole was a few years older than her, but that hadn't put a dent in her deep, high school crush. His family was from the other side of Last Stand—the part that had sprawling ranches and large houses that dated back to the nineteenth century. Nowhere near where she'd grown up in Hickory Creek. Cole had won a ton of regional awards as a bulldogger, but had never made the jump to pro. Her sisters had often teased her about never being around to help them whenever Cole competed. He had been everything her rebellious heart had ever wanted…only, she had always been too chicken to do anything about it.

"I'd love a rum and Coke," she blurted out, reaching down to help him to his feet. Only she accidentally bumped heads with him. "Sorry." April fought hard not to blush. She wished she wasn't so awkward. Apparently, her girlhood crush was still alive and well. He'd always made her nervous.

Cole rubbed his forehead. "Not a problem. Where did Emily and Donovan go?"

April moved so he could get out of the gated area. "They went to grab something to eat. Emily said that we were welcome to join them."

"I'd rather have you all to myself," Cole said. Then, catching himself, he cleared his throat. "To catch up, I mean. It's been a while."

"Yeah," she said breathlessly. A lot had happened since she'd last seen him in high school. Hell, a lot had happened since she'd been let go from her job a month ago. She followed Cole to the bar, feeling like an imposter in her new cowboy boots and borrowed dress. But then again, that was kind of the reason April was here tonight. She'd decided it was well past time she got out of her comfort zone and claimed her spot as a wild Grayson sister.

"Rum and Coke and a large draft beer," he said to the bartender. Cole held out his hand and April took it. Shivers went up her arm and she chastised herself for acting like a fool. But he seemed to feel it too. "Come on, let's get a table."

She let him pull her through the crowd, not quite believing this was actually happening—that she was here in a bar with the man who'd had star billing in all her adolescent fantasies. She sat down across from him, reluctantly letting his hand go. He looked damned good. She was both giddy with nerves and a little punch drunk at the admiration she saw in Cole's eyes.

He had prettiest blue eyes she'd ever seen. They were pale, almost icy blue, but there were laugh lines around them and his mouth. Even though his face was more tanned and weathered than it had been in high school, he was still heart-stoppingly attractive. His once long blond hair was cut short, but his easy grin still charmed her the way it had almost ten years ago. April couldn't tear her gaze away from his, and the heat between them smoldered.

"I haven't seen you around here before. Are you on vacation?" he asked.

"No, I've recently moved back home."

After a lot of angst and planning, April had sublet her apartment in Austin. The money she was saving in rent was helping her keep afloat while she built up her new accounting business. But April Grayson, CPA, hadn't intended to stop there. She was determined to finally let go of the stranglehold she'd had on her life and take a few risks. And tonight was one of them.

"I left for a bit and then came back," he said, leaning back as the waitress brought over their drinks.

"Last Stand will always be home." She smiled up at him, wondering when the butterflies in her stomach would calm down.

"You haven't changed a bit."

April almost snorted, but stopped herself at the last minute. She usually wore her brown hair in a tight bun and preferred her glasses over her contact lenses because her eyes didn't itch so much. Tonight though, her hair was curled and fell softly around her shoulders and she wore more makeup than she ever had. After raiding Merry's closet at Mama's, April had found a fringy club dress that she could wiggle into. It was little bit lower in the chest and higher in the leg than what she was used to, though. She had spent five minutes trying to tug it down before her mother told her to just go and have a good time. April wiggled her toes. Her new cowboy boots pinched, too.

"I'm trying out some new things," she said. "New job. New town. New me."

"I liked the old you."

"Then why didn't you ever ask me out?" April couldn't believe she just blurted that out. Maybe the floor would open and swallow her up.

"Would you have gone out with me if I had?" he countered.

"Of course, I would."

"But you were such a good girl."

"Good girls love bad boys," she said.

"I wasn't that bad." Cole winked at her.

"I wasn't that good."

That was a big fat lie, but he didn't have to know it.

"I've heard about the Grayson sisters. Talk around town is that they're pretty wild," he said with a twinkle in his eye.

April hid a wince. *Great.* Her sisters' reputation preceded her. But then she thought about it. Wasn't that exactly what she wanted?

"You got it, cowboy." She smiled and batted her eyelashes, hoping he wouldn't think she had something in her eye. June and Merry made this look so easy, flirting, and charming men. April had always felt like she was in their shadows, but that was not going to happen tonight. Tonight, she wasn't going to be April Grayson, CPA, known for her sensible shoes and an early bedtime. No, tonight, she was just April, one of the wild Grayson sisters.

Her sisters wouldn't have hesitated to go alone to a bar on a Friday night, and neither would she. Actually, April was thrilled she'd even managed to take the first step—walking in the door, dressed to thrill.

Of course, while the new April was congratulating herself on taking that first step in her wild Grayson transformation, the old April couldn't help quickly going through her list of further things to accomplish.

1. Start her own accounting business: Check! Mr. Jonas had been the first one in line after she'd agreed to give him a major discount for putting up with her mother. Then she'd picked up a few more small businesses. She wasn't making ends meet yet, but she was getting there.

2. Go on a European cruise, alone: Booked! It had almost killed her to put down the deposit when finances were so uncertain, but not being afraid to experience new things was something she really wanted in her life.

3. Overcome her fear of horses: She didn't really want this one on the list. Except it would go a long way to making her feel like she belonged in the same family as her sisters. She'd never be a rodeo queen, but she could stop flinching when a horse was near.

April had hated horses ever since Ares had thrown his head back into her face three times during a barrel race when she was twelve. She supposed she deserved it for naming her horse after the god of war. But after suffering from a concussion, a broken nose and the loss of two teeth, she wasn't in a rush to be anywhere near a horse again.

4. Have a one-night stand: This was a late addition to the list. But she realized that she needed to reclaim her sexuality—on her own terms. And it happened because of a jerk who thought she'd sleep with him just because she was a Grayson. It had been a blind date that she let her mother set her up with to show that she could be spontaneous. It had been a pretty good date. If it had stopped at the end of the movie, she might have gone out with him again. But he had driven to his house, as if it had been a foregone conclusion that they were going to have sex. She'd had to call an Uber while he'd alternatively slut-shamed her and then tried to convince her to "at least" give him a blow job.

Her mother had to be physically restrained from going after him once April told her how the blind date had gone.

The experience had scared April off of dating ever since. But she wasn't that same April anymore, and she wasn't going to let one prick derail her plans. After all, there was nothing wrong with having a one-night stand—she just needed to be choosy about it.

But even before that one guy, her dates had been historically dull. She'd had coffee dates that seldom led to a second. And a few dinner and a movie dates that had eventually fizzled out. She was just too cautious. She'd never wanted to be like Mama, with a different man for every season.

Still, a one-night stand could help her get past all the disappointments. No ties. No expectations. Just good sex. It was certainly wild, and not something she could ever plan.

She was amazed she'd found someone she was interested in so quickly. If she had known she could reconnect with Cole just by wearing fancy dress and having the courage to walk into Buddy's Bar and Boogie all by herself, April would have done it a long time ago.

"Are you on a break from the rodeo?" Cole asked.

That subterfuge could only go so far. She couldn't fake being a rodeo star. "I don't do rodeo. I'm afraid of horses."

"Why?" he said, his mouth hanging open in surprise.

"I had a bad accident when I was a kid." April gave him a brief rundown of what Ares had done to her. "And ever since then, horses and me don't mix."

"I'm sorry to hear that. I spend most of my life in the saddle. What do you do?" he asked.

April didn't really want to tell him that she had been a CPA for one of the biggest accounting firms in Austin. That didn't fit her persona tonight. But she also didn't want to lie. What would June have said? Then, it hit her. April put on a big smile and said, "Anything I want to."

It seemed to work. Cole returned her smile and clinked glasses with her. "That's what I like to hear."

"So, what have you been up to since I last saw you in calculus?" Why had she brought up calculus? Who cared? It was ten years ago, and had been the most boring class on the planet. She'd spent most of her time staring at Cole's wide back and wondering what on earth she could do to get him to notice her. Back then, he had been the poster child for everything April was terrified of. It didn't make her want him any less.

Cole smoked, he drank and he drove his truck way too fast in and out of the school's parking lot. He'd dated lots of girls and threw his daddy's money around like it was confetti. One time, he'd even been busted for running a poker game in the boys' locker room. The only reason he hadn't been expelled was because a few teachers had been playing as well. The episode had been swept under the rug as harmless fun, but even Mama had been scandalized. April would have loved to shock her family by bringing him home for Sunday dinner. Maybe now, she would get the chance.

"I did a bunch of rodeo shows myself," Cole said, bringing her back to the present. "Never went full pro. I wasn't that good. But I won a few purses and had a good time. It helped me get through college."

"What did you study?"

"Teaching and a little social work. But I couldn't quite decide what I wanted to do—I found out I hated being in an office, and a classroom wasn't much better. But I did teach middle school for a while before I got restless."

"What did you do then?" she asked, sighing and wiggling her toes. The rum and Coke was making her a little dizzy, but in a good way.

"I went to Vegas and became a poker player."

"Wow," she said, sloshing her drink. "Sorry." Taking a napkin, she dabbed up the mess. "That sounds exciting." It actually sounded terrifying. Mama had dated several gamblers over the years. It had never ended well.

"It was…until the money ran out."

His smile wasn't so warm anymore. April saw the bleakness in his eyes, and it reminded her of the expressions on her sisters' faces when they realized they had burned through their purse money and couldn't afford gas or upkeep on their horses and trucks. It had taken her years to put them on a budget and to make sure that they automatically socked away twenty percent for taxes. It had been an uphill battle. Cole must have learned that the hard way, too.

One of the gamblers Mama had dated had been from Connecticut. He'd promised to take them all there one summer, and he had. The casinos there looked like palaces buried deep in an enchanted forest. Because they had been underage, she and her sisters had been put in the kids' club while her mother and her boyfriend gambled. At first it had been fun. All the video games they could play and all the pizza they could eat. But after a few hours June had become scared, and it took a long time for the casino employees to track down her mother. Her boyfriend hadn't wanted to leave the roulette table, and she'd stayed by his side, without a thought for her daughters.

Her mother apologized to them over and over again, bought them ice cream and then they all headed back to the room where they spent the next two days while he gambled. It was boring. Her boyfriend lost big and blamed it on them. After they flew back home, they never saw him again. And Mama had lost her entire paycheck so food had been scarce until the following payday. Mama's tips hadn't stretched nearly far enough.

April remembered crying tears of joy when a customer had given Mama twenty bucks for doing her hair. They'd been able to buy staples to get them through. To this day, April couldn't eat oatmeal without wanting to cry.

"That must have been hard," she said sympathetically, though she doubted he'd ever experienced the food insecurity she had.

"I still don't believe it," he said. "I dream sometimes that I'm making a comeback at the table."

"That sounds like a nice dream." The key word being dream, she thought.

Then she mentally shook herself. She couldn't let herself default into CPA mode. Nothing would make Cole lose interest faster. She'd had enough experience with men who'd get a glazed look in their eyes when she'd start talking about finances over dinner.

She drained her rum and Coke, and thumped it back down on the bar.

Cole raised his eyebrow in surprise.

Before she lost courage, she grabbed his hand and said, "Let's dance, cowboy." When April yanked him on the dance floor, the jukebox was playing a fast song, but it seemed as if they'd just got started before it segued into a slow one. Cole pulled her into his arms, and she laid her cheek on the soft cotton of his shirt. At first, April worried about a million things. What if she stumbled or stepped on his toes? Could he hear the racing of her heart? But as the song went on, April relaxed into the easy sway of his hard toned body, and closed her eyes. Dancing with Cole lived up to the fantasy she'd had in high school—that the ultimate bad boy would want the ultimate Goody Two-Shoes. It hadn't happened...but now, it seemed to be close. All she had to do was keep him from realizing that she was a good girl for at least a few more songs.

When the music was over, she blinked up at him dreamily. "That was nice." She leaned up on her tiptoes, intending to brush a kiss on his cheek—a bold move for her. Only she hadn't been expecting Cole to move, and she got him on the lips instead. Tangling his fingers through her hair, he turned what was supposed to have been a sweet peck on the cheek into a full open-mouth kiss.

Well.

Wow.

That was some kiss.

Of course, she had been kissed before, but it had always

been on her terms, in a controlled environment, with clear rules, and a predictable outcome. This kiss was nothing like she'd ever experienced before, and it set her nerves on fire and had her entire body humming with excitement and anticipation for more.

Making out in the middle of the dance floor without worrying about who was watching was an unexpected perk of going wild. Cole's mouth was warm and sweet on hers, and she would have liked nothing better than to continue to kiss him all night long. But as when the jukebox blared out another rocking country song, they were jostled apart by excited dancers setting up for a line dance.

"I've been waiting for that kiss for ten years," he said.

"Me too," she squeaked out.

"Do you want to get out of here?" Cole asked, huskily.

Did she?

Although her plan was to sow some much-needed wild oats, she hadn't planned on taking a stranger home to bed. But Cole wasn't really a stranger. Back in high school, she'd wanted him so badly. But she couldn't believe he'd ever want someone as dull as her. But this was a chance for her to ease that regret. And, of course, there was #4 on her list to think of.

"Yes," she said, before she could change her mind.

"Let's go." With his arm still around her, he guided her toward the door.

She hadn't had a chance to try the mechanical bull, but she had a feeling she was in for a much wilder ride tonight.

"Your place or mine?" he asked.

"Mine," she said. While it probably would be easier to get away if she went to his house, being in her apartment in familiar surroundings made her feel a little bit more in control of the situation. Because nothing about this night had her feeling any control.

That was the point, though, right? Throwing caution to the wind and taking a few risks?

Her head was spinning from his kiss—and maybe from drinking the rum a little too fast. "Wait." Maybe she should take some more time to think this through, to make a list of the pros and cons and weigh each of them individually. But she couldn't say that to Cole. He might get cold feet, and she couldn't take the chance that he'd leave.

Smoothing her hand down her dress, she smiled when his gaze followed. "I think I need a few more dances before I'm all right to drive. That rum really hit me."

The devil on her shoulder, who sounded remarkably like June, said in her ear, *"Don't think! Just go for it! He's a hot man and you're a willing woman. Ride 'em, cowgirl!"*

The devil on her other shoulder sounded just like herself—when she was in overthinking mode—rattling on endlessly in her ear, *"Is he married? Is this a date? Will he respect you? Do you want to see him again? What if it's just the liquor talking? What if it's not any good? What if this is a terrible idea?"*

Cole rubbed her arm, bringing her back from the dizzying indecision. "I'm moving too fast. I'm sorry. It's just that you're so damned beautiful. I lost my head."

Beautiful. He called her beautiful. She smiled up at him.

"It's not that. I just don't do this a lot." *At all.* "Do you mind if we ease off the gas? Just a bit."

"I don't mind at all." He flashed a sexy grin.

April sagged in relief. While the boring part of her might have been hoping he would turn her down so she'd have time to come back to her senses, April realized that she didn't want that. She'd earned her wild night out with the cowboy of her dreams. She just needed a few more minutes to come to terms with what she was about to do. And to start thinking of ways to make sure he never, ever forgot her.

Chapter Four

C OLE PULLED HER around the dance floor for the next several songs. They laughed and danced until her feet were too sore to do anything but slink back to their booth. He was a great dancer and she'd even learned a line dance or two. They ordered a platter of chicken sliders and fries and dug in.

"What's a nice guy like you doing all alone on a Friday night?" April asked. She had already checked out the ring finger on his left hand. Nothing. Not even a tan line that would show where a ring would've been.

"I needed a break, change of scenery."

"I understand that." April chugged down a large glass of water. Though she would have preferred beer, she needed to be clear-headed for what came next. "Hard week?"

"I've had worse." His face clouded over for a moment, but then he smiled again. "How about you?"

"I'm still settling into my apartment. I've got a job interview on Monday."

Cole clinked water glasses with her. "Good luck. Where is it?"

She hesitated to tell him that her interview was with

Trent Campbell at the Three Sisters Ranch. He was also a bit of a local hero in Last Stand, like her sisters. The last thing April wanted to do was to talk about horses and rodeos. She wasn't really a fan of either, although Cole's rope work had been fascinating to watch.

Fortunately, she was saved from having to answer when the waitress came over with a game console. "Hey, are you guys interested in competing in trivia night tonight?"

"Depends," Cole drawled. "What are the stakes?"

"The winners get a pair of tickets to see Rocking Randy Roy and his band play here next Saturday."

"We're in," April said, scooting closer to Cole so they sat shoulder to shoulder in the booth.

He hooked an arm around her as she set up the game with their names.

As the waitress cleared their empty dishes away, she asked, "Can I get you something to drink?"

"Diet Coke, please," April said. "I'm going to need caffeine to keep me sharp."

"I'll take a root beer," Cole said.

"I'm really good at trivia," April said, grinning up at him.

He kissed her quickly on the lips, and that tingling energy strummed through her again.

"Then, we'll make a good team. I'm a font of useless information."

She pressed closer to him, enjoying his warmth.

As they answered the questions, Cole trailed his fingers over her bare arm. April shivered and indulged in a few more of his sweet kisses. Before long, the game was nearly forgotten, something that would have appalled her at the beginning of the night. She was competitive, probably too competitive, but she was having a hard time concentrating and it showed in their dismal score.

"I was distracted," she said when they came in a disappointing third place.

"Complaining?" Cole tilted her chin up with his fingers and kissed her.

She could get used to this. His lips were velvety soft and oh-so-lickable. "Not at all."

"Are you still up for tonight?" he asked.

"You bet." Her head was clear of any fuzziness that the rum might have left behind. Any trepidation she'd felt was now gone, and an overwhelming desire to spend the night with Cole filled her. She took out her keys. "Why don't you follow me home?"

"Will you keep me, if I do?" Cole said, signaling the waitress for their check.

That made her think of the barn kittens that June would beg her mother to keep. "He followed me home," she'd say. "Can I keep him?"

"I might." April was tempted to jump up and yell, *"Yes! This is happening."* She was finally going to have a wild adventure.

Cole kissed her again in the parking lot, a little more urgently this time and with a lot more steam. His mouth seduced hers until she was needy and restless. She wasn't sure how long they stood there, kissing. Time had seemed to stop when he'd pressed her up against his truck. But it wasn't enough. She needed more. Fumbling with the handle, she opened the passenger-side door.

"C'mere," April muttered, tugging him inside the cab.

Thank God for bench seats.

After Cole closed the door, she wiggled around so she could straddle his lap, though they never stopped kissing. April was shaking with the need to touch him. Fumbling with the buttons on his shirt, she barely noticed when a few of them went flying. Finally, her fingers were on his bare chest.

"Slow down, baby," he panted as she shimmied the dress over her head.

"Can't," she said and leaned in to kiss him again. Then a spark of rationality hit her. "Unless, you don't want to?" A slight chill filled the warm cab and April started to cross her arms over her chest. What was she doing? This wasn't her. And yet, she didn't want to stop.

Cole gently lifted her arms away and kissed the inside of her wrists. April shivered as her nipples puckered into hard aching points. "Oh, I want to." He unhooked her bra. "I just want to take some time to enjoy you."

He cupped her breasts and brought them to his hot mouth. April steadied herself with both hands on the roof of his truck and rocked herself against his jean-clad erection. Biting her lip, she tossed her head back as he sucked hard on one nipple.

"Do you like that?" Cole swirled his tongue around it.

"Oh yeah," she breathed and ground against him.

He caressed his hand down her arching back and into her

panties. April held his head to her breast while he gripped her ass. She couldn't stop moving against his delicious hardness. The lights in the parking lot spun around as she picked up the pace.

"That's it, sweetness," he moaned. "Use me to get off."

His words thrilling her almost as much as his talented mouth on her breasts, April gave out a sharp cry as pleasure thrummed through her. Her breasts rubbed over his face and when he ripped her panties off, April clung to him while she fell apart.

Holy shit that was hot.

"Do you have a condom?" he asked, laying her back on the seat.

"In my purse," she panted weakly, pointing where it had fallen on the floor.

Tossing it to her, he folded her legs back and put his tongue inside her.

"Cole," she shrieked, her toes hitting the driver-side window. She was almost bent in two, but all she could feel was him licking her to another fast orgasm. Cole's five-o'clock shadow rasped against her thighs and made for sweet friction as he got serious about what he was doing. Groping for the condom, April stared up at the ceiling of the truck in surprise. My God! This, *this*, was what she had been missing all these years, dating nice accountant men? She should have been with bad-boy cowboys—this bad-boy cowboy in particular.

"You're gorgeous," he said, huskily.

She barely could control the sounds that were coming

out of her mouth, and when she came again, her entire body shook from the force of it.

"Cole," she purred, watching him pull his jeans down over his hips. She wanted to lick every inch of him, but she could barely move.

"You're the hottest thing I've ever seen," he said, plucking the condom out of her nerveless fingers.

Her mouth was dry as she watched him slowly unroll the condom onto his thick, hard cock. Pulling her up, he lifted her on his lap. April felt boneless, but was able to help guide him inside her. Cole pulled her down on top of him, engulfing himself completely.

She lost herself in his blue eyes. This felt right. She tightened around him and his eyes closed. He hitched in his breath and held her still.

April pouted and made a small sound of impatience.

"I'm closer than I thought, darlin'," he said.

"You don't have to go slow for me," April whispered into his ear. "I like it a little rough."

He groaned. "You're going to kill me." Brushing aside her hair, Cole buried his face in her neck. "You smell so good and you feel like heaven."

He nibbled at her throat and rubbed her breasts, plucking her nipples. April held him close and slid herself up and down his shaft. She rubbed her body against his, loving the way he growled softly against her skin. Then Cole ultimately gave in to his desire, grabbing her hips and thrust up. Losing her balance, she could only cling desperately to him as he took them both on a hard and fast ride.

April laughed and moaned in pleasure, unsure of the swirling emotions going on inside her. She felt wild and free and completely unlike herself. And she loved it.

"You're everything I ever dreamed of," she cried out, digging her nails deep into his shoulders. This fantasy was perfect. *He* was perfect.

His teeth nipped down at the sweet spot at the juncture of her throat and she came apart again. Cole held her, as she thrashed and sobbed in pleasure, while he continued to thrust into her with hard, controlled strokes. When she was finally reduced to shaky whimpers, he growled his climax and claimed her mouth with a deep kiss.

Moments later, April opened her eyes and looked around. Sex in a truck was exciting…until it was over. She suddenly realized she was naked in a parking lot for the entire bar to see if they decided to peer into the steamed-up windows. Embarrassed, she couldn't look at Cole as he placed her onto the passenger side of the truck and took care of the condom. Luckily, she found her dress and wiggled into it. Her bra and panties were a lost cause.

Cole eased himself back into his jeans, but his shirt gaped where the buttons were missing.

"Sorry," she said, reaching over to try and fix it.

"Worth it," he said. "Totally."

It had been. But now that the endorphins had cooled, April was all too aware that she wasn't one of her sisters. There was casual sex and then there was having your world rocked in the cab of a Ford F250. She wasn't a teenager. She should at least have waited until they got back to her apartment.

Where the hell were her keys?

She must have spotted them at the same time Cole did because they knocked heads bending down, reaching for them.

"Sorry," he said, rubbing his forehead.

"It's okay; maybe it knocked some sense into me," April said ruefully, fiddling with her keys.

"Oh?" Cole cocked his head. "Did I do something wrong?"

"No," she rushed to reassure him. "It's not you. It's me." April grimaced. Did she really say that?

AWK-WARD.

"Look, this was fun. It was great." Now, she was babbling. "I should go. Thanks. For everything." April squeezed his arm and opened the truck door.

"Are you sure I can't make it up to you?" Cole asked.

She had no idea what the hell he was talking about, but the cool night air reminded her that her panties were in shreds on the floor of his truck. April didn't know whether to be mortified or proud, so instead she settled on confused. Her heart was racing and she was afraid of doing something wrong. She really liked Cole, but after tonight, she didn't have enough courage to turn around and ask for his number.

"I'll see you around," she said instead, and closed the truck door.

Hurrying to her car, she half-hoped that he would follow her, while the sane part of her was glad he didn't. What a mess. She got into the driver's seat and locked the door.

Looking around the parking lot, she wondered if anyone had spied on them. Her face burned in embarrassment, but also a little bit of excitement.

"Drive up to his window and get his number," the devil on one shoulder said.

"Quit while you're ahead," said the overthinking angel on her other shoulder.

This time, she listened to it.

Chapter Five

C OLE LOVED HIS job, but he was having a hard time getting into the swing of Monday morning. He'd been so damned tired this morning, he'd been tempted to roll over and go back to sleep. But since he lived above his place of work, that wouldn't fly. It was his own fault really. He had stayed up too late playing online poker. But he ended his session five thousand dollars ahead.

Still, it didn't make him any less groggy as he hauled himself downstairs and went through the daily opening procedures at Trent Campbell's Rodeo School. Hell, he had to read the day's schedule three times until it finally made sense. But he'd get through it. He always did. While he waited for his coffee to brew, he reluctantly plopped down at his desk and fired up his computer.

Cole was proud to be working with Trent, teaching kids about taking care of themselves and their horses while doing fun things like winning blue ribbons and trophies in the local rodeos. Any time that he could raise a kid's self-esteem, he felt a little better about his own life choices. Still, there were days when he questioned himself.

Should he have gone for a life on the back of a horse?

But his back and legs weren't what they used to be ten years ago, and now that he was looking thirty in the face, he knew he'd made the right choice, even if he was a little bored.

One of the good things about sitting behind the desk during the day was it gave him some time to relax. During the evenings, he had his hands full at his second job, hauling bales of hay, and driving a tractor around.

Unfortunately, with both his parents being ill, Cole needed to have as many streams of income as possible to help with the medical bills and for their home health care worker. Gwen was worth every penny of her salary, but sometimes he had to skip a bill payment to make sure she was paid.

Restless, Cole left the small office that he was going to share with the accountant and went back into the kitchenette to see if glaring at the coffee maker made it go any faster. When his phone rang, he fumbled around before he realized it was in his back pocket.

"Hello," he said.

"Cole, can you stop by this morning?" his mother asked.

"Is everything all right?" He pushed down the flare of alarm that went through him. Thelma Lockwood never asked for anything, from anyone. She prided herself on being capable of handling any and all emergencies.

She sighed. "Your father is having problems with the lawn mower."

It was barely eight a.m. His father should have been in bed, recovering from his latest round of chemotherapy.

"Where's Gwen?" Cole asked.

"She won't be here until later."

"So why is he messing with the lawn mower now?"

"Oh, you know your father."

Yes, he certainly did. When his father had sold his cattle and most of the pastures, he'd planned to retire and enjoy his golden years. That had lasted maybe six months. Until he had taken sick, he had made a regular pest of himself around the house and gardens.

"He's not planning on mowing, is he?"

"I don't think so," his mother said, but she didn't sound too sure.

Biting back a curse, he looked at the clock. "I can't get away for another hour. Do what you can to keep him off it."

"I know. I'll make him a big breakfast."

He didn't like the idea of his mother puttering around the kitchen all by herself either. She'd become very frail after her latest gall bladder operation. But she'd had the time to recover and had had the good sense to stay in bed during her convalescence.

"I'll send over a tray of pancakes and sausage from the Bluebonnet Diner."

"They deliver now?" she asked.

"Yeah." Cole didn't have the time to explain to her about the various delivery services that all of the local restaurants were using these days.

"That's handy."

The bell over the front door of the school tinkled.

"Mom, I've got to go. Someone's here. I'll stop by on my lunch break."

He reluctantly walked past the coffee maker and went

out to meet whoever had come in. To Cole's surprise, it was his boss. Trent was limping slightly and not using his cane, which would have driven his wife, Kelly, nuts if she'd seen him.

"You're in early," Cole said.

"I've got an interview with one of the Grayson sisters today."

Cole's libido woke up and he turned back around to get that cup of coffee. "What for?" It had to be April. She had told him about having a job interview this morning. Maybe he'd be able to apologize for his behavior Friday night. He should have taken her home or gone to her place. He hadn't meant to be so disrespectful of her in the truck, but she had him so crazy, he hadn't been able to think straight.

"The accountant position."

Cole blinked at his boss in disbelief. "One of the Grayson sisters? An accountant?"

"She came highly recommended," Trent Campbell said. "Why?"

Cole rubbed his hand over his face. "They're not known for staying in one place very long." *And I might have had sex with her in my truck Friday night.*

"All those rumors about them can't possibly be true," Trent said.

"Are all those rumors about you true?"

Trent winced. "More or less."

But that was many years in the past. Now, Trent was a devoted husband to Kelly Sullivan Campbell, whose family owned the Three Sisters Ranch where Trent's business was situated. And the former rodeo star was now an adoring father to their daughter, Alissa, and they had another little girl on the way.

"April is a CPA and she got a glowing recommendation from her old firm in Austin," Trent said, walking with care into Cole's soon-to-be-shared office.

Cole blew out a sigh. It *was* April. Should he tell Trent about their hot one-night stand? On the one hand, it really wasn't any of his boss's business. On the other hand, he didn't want things to get weird. After April had taken him for one hell of a ride on Friday, she'd scurried away like she was ashamed or something. He'd been too shocked at her sudden departure to get her number. Cole would have been more than happy to follow her home so he could make it up to her for being so damned quick, but he had gotten the impression that she wouldn't have wanted that.

There was no sense berating himself about that now. He'd made his bed and now he had to lie in it. Or in the case of the delectable April Grayson, his truck bed—although his front seat had seen all the action. He inwardly groaned. A gentleman really should have seen her home at the very least, but there had been nothing gentlemanly about the way he'd felt when she had been pressed up against him. He wondered if he should tell Trent that he might have a problem working in the same small office with April. He knew without a doubt that his concentration would be shot to hell.

Cole had been worried that night about the way she had taken off, and he had wanted to make sure she was all right, so he did some investigating on the Grayson sisters. There was surprisingly nothing about April anywhere. June was reported to be out with an injury, and Merry was talking about retiring. At least, that's what the scuttlebutt was.

"A CPA?" Cole knew he was probably being stereotypical, but April didn't resemble any accountant that he'd ever seen. She looked like the rodeo queen of his dreams. He took a long swallow of the hot coffee to keep his imagination from running wild.

"Do you know April?" Trent asked.

Cole hoped his expression didn't give him away. "We've met."

"Do you like her?"

Hell yeah. "She's a great girl. I didn't know she was an accountant. I had her pegged as something more..." *Wild, exotic, free-spirited.* Cole shrugged.

The hell of it was, he wished he had met her several years ago, before real life had crashed down on him. Last Friday night had been a rare treat for him. He had only gone to Buddy's because the high-stakes game he'd intended to join had fallen through. That fact still annoyed the crap out of him. He was sure he could have at least paid off the anesthesiologist's bill or put a dent in the facility charge, if he'd won a few hands. Cole just wished that his parents' insurance had covered more of their doctors' bills.

"Do you think she's going to be a problem, Cole?" Trent asked. "Her sisters aren't really PG-rated no matter how hard they've tried to clean up their acts. We've got a lot of kids around here."

"Nah, she'll be fine." Cole shook his head. They'd been

drinking. It had been a hot time, and things tended to get crazy at Buddy's anyway. It was like Vegas. What happened at the bar, stayed at the bar.

Speaking of Vegas, he pulled out his phone and looked at the poker tournament schedule. He could make more in one night in a poker game then he could all month at all his jobs combined. If his luck held out.

Luck or skill? He loved playing poker, because it was the only excitement he had in his otherwise dull life these days. Oh sure, watching one of the kids finally stay on a horse or a bull after hours of trying was a rush, but it wasn't the same 'sitting at a table with a bunch of sharks that walked on two legs, and coming out ahead' type of rush. Although sexy April Grayson had come close to that level. If they'd had more time, Cole was positive she would have exceeded it.

"So do you think she'll work out? I've got five years of taxes that need to be put to bed. I'm sick of getting extensions to avoid dealing with the paperwork mess. And I need someone to find me the most deductions possible." Trent scowled at the stacks of boxes that were piled up by the spare desk and spilling out into the hallway.

"You said she came highly recommended. Go with your gut after you interview her." Cole thought that she would do the job she was hired for, but if something more interesting than Last Stand called her name, he just hoped that she'd do right by Trent before she took off. "I'm going to check on the animals," Cole said, leaving Trent sifting hopelessly through the copier paper boxes of records. "Do you mind if I take off for a bit afterward? My parents are having some issues."

Trent looked up from the receipts. "Is everything all right?"

"My dad's trying to do yard work and my mom's still too fragile to hog-tie him to a chair."

Smirking, Trent tossed the paperwork back. "We should get him and Frank together."

Frank Sullivan's name was on the deed to the Three Sisters Ranch, but his three daughters managed all five thousand acres of it. Frank was supposed to be taking it easy after his two heart attacks almost took his life. If it hadn't been for Kelly, Janice and Emily, the Three Sisters Ranch would have gone on the auction block.

"I think that would be a bad idea. They might gang up on us," Cole said.

Mock shuddering, Trent said, "I can't even imagine. Sure, take as much time as you need. Billy is coming over before lunch. He can pitch in if you're not back in time for your classes."

Billy King was Trent's father and former manager. He helped out around the school when he wasn't busy with his other rodeo clients. Cole thought he did it to keep an eye out for future rodeo stars as much as he did it to help his son. "I'll be back before the classes start."

Cole was in his element when the students were there and he could work with them one-on-one on the horses or on the small bulls—and for the real little kids, the sheep. In fact, mutton busting was one of the favorite activities on the Three Sisters Ranch. Sometimes Kelly would come out and take pictures of the little soon-to-be cowpokes. If the families wanted more formal portraits, she charged them, but the candid shots were one of the perks for enrolling at Trent's school.

"You're going to miss April Grayson," Trent called after him as Cole headed for the barns.

Maybe it was better if he wasn't there for the interview. Cole didn't want her to be nervous.

He was eager to see April again, even if she didn't want to pick up where they left off. It would be good to look across the desk and see a pretty friendly face instead of the same four walls. Not that he spent a lot of time at his desk... But for April, he'd make an exception.

Chapter Six

APRIL WAS BACK in accountant mode as Trent Campbell gave her the tour of his rodeo school. Her sisters would have loved to have been here right now. Trent was a local Last Stand hero. He had put his life on the line riding the same crazed bull that had ended his rodeo career, in order to win a humongous purse to help the Three Sisters Ranch stave off bankruptcy.

And he'd done it all for love. It was so romantic. Kelly—one of her best friends and Trent's wife—was blissfully happy. Then again, she deserved to be, after all the shit her father put her through. Unfortunately, she was having a hard pregnancy and April was trying not to be worried sick about her. She'd made sure to stock up on tea and cookies from the Austin tea shop before she left, so Kelly could have her supplies.

If Merry and June had been here, April would have used Trent as an example of what to do after the rodeo took its toll on you. She worried that her sisters wouldn't be able to find fulfillment if they weren't on the road, traveling from one event to the other, cross country and back. Trent seemed to be doing just fine staying in one place. He had a big house, a beautiful wife and daughter and he seemed really happy.

Emily might also be a good influence on her younger sister. June and Emily had been BFFs in high school, and they had kept in touch when Emily had gone into the Peace Corps and June had joined the rodeo circuit. Maybe Emily could get June to settle down a bit. She was partying way too much lately. Even Merry said so.

"What was your event?" Trent asked her as an older man led a group of kids in a rope lesson outside. They were trying to rope sawhorses, while in the distance, a group of real horses lazed around the paddock. "I don't remember you barrel racing with your sisters."

"I was more of a support team member. When we were little, Mama drove the truck and I planned out the routes. You couldn't pay me to get on a horse or a bull. No offense," she added.

"None taken," Trent said good-naturedly, steering her around a pile of horse manure that she almost stepped in.

Good thing he did. She was wearing her new navy pumps.

"So, you were the navigator," he confirmed as he led her toward the main building of the school.

"The navigator, the stall cleaner, the warden." She smirked, remembering her siblings' reactions to the few times she'd had to insist they eat ramen and bologna sandwiches for dinner instead of going out for a steak and fries.

"Warden? Wasn't that more your mother's job?"

April snorted. "She's almost as bad as my sisters. I've

controlled the checkbook since I was sixteen. I loved it when I could set the bills up to be paid automatically every month. No more having the lights turned off."

"That must have been tough with all the traveling your sisters did."

"When we were all in school, it was easier. But after high school, it turned into a free-for-all. I took online college courses instead of going somewhere because I was worried about the trouble they'd get into if I wasn't there, pulling back on the reins."

"That must have been tough."

"It was. But it was fun too. Merry and June are so talented. And I love my family. Being together meant the world to me."

"Why aren't you still out there with them then?" he asked.

"They grew up and Mama got sick of traveling. They have the routine down and know that I'll audit their accounts to make sure they're socking away enough for retirement and taxes."

"And if you find them skimming?"

"Oh, then there'll be hell to pay."

"So the wild Grayson sisters are afraid of you? I think that's pretty badass." Trent grinned.

She stumbled and had to reach out and grab his arm to steady herself. "I hadn't thought about it that way."

"The gossip is that Merry is looking to retire. You have her set up for that?"

April barked out a laugh. "Oh hell, no. She's got to work

until she's sixty-five or so like the rest of us. But it doesn't have to be on the back of the horse, if she doesn't want to."

"Smart. I wish I had someone like you during my younger days." He glanced back toward the pen. "I had Billy with me, though. I did all right. Except for the taxes part."

"I'm sure I can help with that," April said, feeling excited about the prospect.

Inside the bull-riding school, there was a gymnasium with the bull-riding machines on top of thick padded mats. They were the more sophisticated versions of the barrel her mother had strung up between some trees that she and her sisters had played on in the front yard of the trailer park. She probably couldn't stay on these ones for any length of time either, even if Merry wasn't there, trying her hardest to dump her off.

Trent's office was down the hallway. An entire wall was a picture window that looked out into the pasture. Luckily, she didn't see any horses out there. April stifled a shudder. Still, there was one ornery-looking bull that gave her the stink eye as it wandered by the window.

"Don't mind Red, there," Trent said as they sat down at his desk. "My daughter wanted to name him Flower Bud and he's never gotten over the insult."

April giggled. "Well, I don't blame him. Although I don't know if Red is any better. Are you getting paid endorsements for having him out there?"

"I should." Trent eased himself into his chair and massaged his leg.

"Are you all right?" she asked.

"Broke my leg in three places. It aches a bit when it's going to rain." He shrugged. "Anyway, I'm not one for long interviews, ma'am."

"April, please," she said. Did she really look like a ma'am?

"April." Trent smiled. "Your résumé is very impressive."

"Thank you," April said, feeling a little surge of pride. She had earned it.

"Are you comfortable doing past taxes and delayed filings?"

April nodded. "That was the bulk of what I did in Austin."

"Are you looking for a permanent position? Because I'm afraid I'm only looking to hire someone temporarily to get my books in order."

"That would work out for me. I've decided to start up my own business instead of working for another big accounting firm. I hope to take on some local clients in the Last Stand and Whiskey River areas." And her landing this job would go a long way for word-of-mouth references.

"So you wouldn't be exclusive to me for this tax season? There's a lot of work. I've been..." He cleared his throat. "A little lax with my record keeping." Trent frowned slightly. "I made you up a desk in the other office."

Uh-oh, I'd better fix this, because it sounds like he wants to hire me.

"I won't need to be exclusive. However, in the first month or so, I'll be happy to work onsite to get you organized and prepared for this year's taxes as well as all the back filings. And I'd be available whenever you needed me."

"I apologize in advance. My receipts are a mess. My personal tax forms and the business are all mixed up." He shrugged. "I'm a cowboy. I do the best when I'm out with the horses. Not when I'm inside at a desk."

"I understand," April said. "I'm the same way, only just the opposite."

"I'd like to offer you the job, but I think you should see what you're getting into first before saying yes."

April resisted doing a little dance of glee when she stood up to follow Trent into the other office.

"You'll be sharing the office with my youth director, Cole Lockwood."

April nearly slammed into Trent's back. *Hold the phone. Cole Lockwood? As in my one and only one-night stand. What have I gotten myself into?*

"Is there a problem?" Trent asked, cocking his head quizzically.

"No," she said quickly, shaking her head. "Don't mind me."

"You know Cole, right? He mentioned it this morning."

Panic flared through her. "He did? What did he say?"

"Just that you met. He's sorry that he couldn't be here, but his parents are ill and he's their only support."

Holding her hand over her wildly beating heart, April tried to calm herself from the panic brought on by wondering what Cole had said. As long as he hadn't mentioned truck sex, everything should be fine.

"I'm sorry to hear about his parents."

"He's been working himself ragged."

"Are you sure Cole isn't going to mind sharing his office?" Her heart refused to settle down at the thought of working in the same room as Cole. Would he treat her like a coworker? Or more? Could there actually be a chance she could date him for real? She started to get a little light-headed at the thought.

"No," Trent said. "With everything going on, he's barely at his desk."

That figured. Oh well, maybe it was for the best.

"He's my youth activities director. He works with the kids, showing them the basics—from roping, to ways of keeping their seat in the saddle, and how to take care of the equipment. There's a lot of stall cleaning at that age, as you can imagine. I hope you don't mind the smell."

"I remember. I'm sure I'll either get used to it or learn to close the windows. Where do you keep your files and tax paperwork?"

Trent flushed and cleared his throat. He inclined his head to the desk on the right. "I don't really have a formal filing system, but those boxes contain the last seven years. I'm only behind for five of them, but the other two years' worth will show you what I've done in the past. But they're in no particular order. Sorry."

Oh my.

April felt her face blanch, but then she straightened her spine. She was always up for a challenge and she was certainly qualified. "That's not a problem," she forced herself to say.

Recovering, she looked at the two desks that were pushed

up to face each other. On one side there were piles of paperwork and large copier boxes stacked waist-high. The other side was Cole's.

Her gaze slid over to his neat desk. Aside from a coffee cup and a computer, there wasn't much there to mark the desk as his. A few small certificates from his rodeo days were hung up behind the chair. And while there was no floor-to-ceiling window like Trent's, the two windows in the office were more than enough to let in a cool breeze.

"Have I scared you off?" Trent asked in a quiet voice.

"Nope, not at all. I'm confident I can get you caught up and filed in no time. Then I'll set you up with a system so filing next year's taxes will be a breeze."

"Sounds good to me. Let's talk salary over a cup of coffee."

April followed him to the little kitchenette and sat at the small table. After about a half hour of chitchat, they came up with a satisfactory figure for both of them.

"When would you like me to start?" April asked.

"How about now?" Trent said. "Although tomorrow, you'll probably want to wear jeans and boots around here. I'd hate to have your fancy clothes get dirty from all the dust the animals—and kids—kick up."

She could hardly wait.

Chapter Seven

A LL THE LAWN mower needed was a spark plug and air filter change, but Cole felt better that he'd taken a look at it after he'd come over to deliver his parents' breakfast in person. Then he'd stayed until Gwen had started her shift.

"Give me a call if you need me," he said.

"Don't worry about us." Gwen had already settled his father on the couch with the Cowboy Channel on. And his mother was busy with her magazines and her cross-stitch.

As he lingered in the doorway, some of the anxiety in his chest loosened at seeing them getting back to normalcy. The last year had been hell on them, and the bills were starting to pile up. Cole ran his hand over the new construction that made it easier for his parents to live all on one floor, so he didn't have to worry about them navigating the stairs when he wasn't around.

Looking up at the second floor longingly, Cole wondered if he could get away with a quick nap before heading back to work. Of course, given how tired he was, he'd sleep the day away. And he couldn't do that to Trent.

As he was driving back to the Three Sisters Ranch, he got the call he'd been waiting for since Friday. Cole answered it on Bluetooth, squeezing the steering wheel in an effort to keep the anger out of his voice.

"Hello, Vic," he said.

"I know you're pissed, but hear me out."

Cole didn't say anything, which Vic took as encouragement. "The Longhorn Club got raided on Thursday."

That didn't surprise him. The Longhorn Club had a ten percent rake and that was illegal in Texas. What did surprise him was after the frantic call he got on Friday morning—the one telling him that the game was off and to stay tuned for more information—nobody, not Vic nor any of the other fixers, had been in touch to reschedule.

"Can't we do this at a private residence?" Without the rake—the money that the house took as a percentage of the pot—Cole could bet more and not worry about having to share his winnings.

"Are you offering up your daddy's place?"

"Hell no." If his parents had been well, Cole might have taken the risk. Back when he was in Vegas and everyone was healthy, his parents rarely used the first floor unless they were entertaining. They would have loved for him to host "his friends" for poker night. Of course, if they knew the poker chips were markers for real cash, they might have had second thoughts. High-stakes games like the one Cole was dying to get into were dangerous, because there was always a chance someone would try and rob the players. A club had its own security to take care of that. But the owners of the Longhorn Club had become greedy and had wanted a piece of the action.

"You and everyone else," Vic grumbled. "It's getting harder and harder to find a venue."

"So when's the next game?" With the five thousand dollars he had won last night, Cole had a total of ten thousand dollars burning a hole in his pocket. He'd like to triple it if he could, to get some traction on the medical bills that were hanging over his family's head. Ten thousand wouldn't even make a dent in them. He needed a game to make the money work for him instead of just sitting in a bank account collecting dust.

"Not until things die down here."

"Damn it." Cole tightened his hands on the wheel in frustration.

"Why don't you go down to Vegas?"

Cole had enough cash to get into a ring game—a non-tournament one—in Vegas. But unfortunately, he didn't have the time off available. "I can't get away." He stared out the windshield at the ranches he drove by. Maybe some of them needed an extra hand. The trouble was he was running out of hours in the day to do the work. He didn't think he could fit in a third job.

"All right. Sorry, man. I'll call you when I hear something."

"Thanks," Cole grumbled and disconnected the call.

Trent was actually going to Vegas later this month to look at some bull stock at a rodeo they were having out there. Maybe Cole could convince Trent to bring him along as company. It would take the sting out of missing his night jobs if he was getting paid to be in Vegas and got his plane ticket and hotel comped by the rodeo school. But that was unlikely. Money was tight all around. And Cole no longer had the clout at the casinos there to get a free ride.

His mother's gall bladder surgery had led to complications, which had resulted in bills that had nearly wiped out their retirement savings. His father's cancer had finished off what little money they'd had left. Cole's salary from the school was keeping them afloat and his night job was paying Gwen's salary. But the bills kept coming.

If he had done better on the circuit, won more purses, they might not have been in this situation. If he had been a better poker player, he might still be in Vegas, paying their bills from his winnings. For five years, he slept all day and played poker all night. He'd had lines of credit in all the major Las Vegas casinos. He'd been considering traveling up north to check out the Indian casinos when his luck had flatlined. Suddenly, he'd lost his touch and Cole wasn't sure what exactly had gone wrong. Had he become too cocky? Was he taking too much for granted?

Unfortunately, he'd never had a chance to make a comeback. When his parents had become ill, he'd left Vegas and come home to Last Stand. He had been lucky to score the job teaching the grade school kids how to ride and rope, but there would always be a part of him that would wonder if he could have weathered the storm and come back from his slump.

Instead, he was a broke cowboy with more problems than he could afford. He was one injury away from bankruptcy and the futility of it was almost enough to make him smash his fist through his windshield. But all that would get him was another bill and a broken hand.

"Crap," Cole said, as he got out of the truck. He was late and Billy was in the middle of his class. Not wanting to distract the kids, he just acknowledged Billy with a grateful wave and went inside to apologize to Trent.

Only Trent wasn't there. But in Cole's office, there was a flurry of activity. Leaning against the doorframe, Cole smiled for the first time that day. April rocked a power suit with some serious sensible shoes that did nothing to hide how fantastic her legs looked. A flash of heat went straight to his groin when he remembered settling in between those legs. Cole swallowed hard when he realized he could carry her upstairs to his room, and have a second chance to make a good impression.

"Hey," he said, his voice huskier than usual.

"Oh!" April fumbled with the folder she had just pulled out of a cardboard box. She managed to clasp it to her before the papers went everywhere. "You startled me."

"Sorry about that. Carry on." He went to his desk and eased into his seat. He needed to send in some applications to the junior league rodeo society for his kids. It was a charity organization that gave out equipment to kids who needed it.

He caught her staring at him a few times under her eyelashes. "Something you want to talk about?" he drawled.

She huffed out a sigh and closed the office door.

"Easy boy!" he told his libido as his mind filled in a bunch of scenarios.

"I wanted to apologize for running away like I did after... Well, after." She clasped her hands in front of her.

"I'll accept your apology as long as you accept mine for not waiting until we got back to your place." Her blush enchanted him.

"I wasn't exactly helpful in that area," she said with a bashful smile that made him want to kiss her senseless again.

"I'm not complaining. I'm just looking for another chance to do it right this time."

"Really?"

This time the folder in her hands dropped and the papers spilled all over the floor. He got up to help her pick them up, making sure they were far enough away so that they didn't bonk heads this time.

"Why on earth does that surprise you?" he asked after they rescued the papers. He knew he was standing too close to her, but he couldn't help himself. She smelled like sunshine and he wanted to taste her lips again.

"I'm not really a wild Grayson sister," she stammered, placing her hand on his chest to steady herself. Her little palm was warm against him...and definitely not enough. "But I want to be."

That startled him out of his thoughts. "What do you mean?"

"This is all so new to me, seducing men in their trucks." Her smile was too self-deprecating for his liking.

"I thought I was seducing you?"

April stepped away and he forced himself not to follow her and press her against the wall, but it was tough. "You did. You still are."

"If I'm making you feel uncomfortable, I'll stop." He deliberately went back to his desk and sat down. "In this office, things will be strictly business between us, if that's what you want."

"It is," she said. "But outside of it, we can pick up where we left off, if that's what you want." April bit her lip in indecision.

"I do want," he said. "Very much. In fact, what time do you finish today?"

"I was going to call it a day at three, but I think I'll stay until I can get this sorted. That way, I'll be able to really dig into it tomorrow."

Then it hit him. He couldn't take her out to dinner. He had to be at the Braxton farm tonight. They needed him to fill in with some barn chores until about ten or so. In fact, that's what his schedule looked like until the weekend. Taking a glance at his calendar, he saw that he had the afternoon free on Saturday, sort of.

"I'm kinda busy this week, but the Sullivan family is having a picnic on Saturday at the ranch house. Everyone's invited. I'd love to introduce you to everyone."

"I'd like that," she said, going back to her files.

"And then afterward, we could come back here if you'd like. I live in the apartment upstairs."

April looked at the ceiling. After a few minutes, in such a low voice Cole thought he imagined it, she added, "Maybe we could take a long lunch sometime too."

Chapter Eight

WORKING IN THE same office as Cole this week had been sheer bliss. Sorting through Trent's tax paperwork—not so much. By the end of the week, April had finally gotten the five years sorted into their correct file boxes and was now going through them to make sure that nothing was going to come back and bite Trent in the ass with an audit. Then she had to file the five years of taxes that Trent still needed to file.

Aside from a sweet tension between them, Cole was the perfect gentleman. He remembered how she liked her coffee and often brought her a cup while they were working. April packed an extra sandwich for him because she noticed he usually worked through lunch or went upstairs for a quick nap instead of eating. She hadn't drummed up the courage yet, though, to ask if he'd like her to join him. Although Cole was out of the office more than he was in it, April found herself looking out the window, watching him working with the kids. He was so great with them, her ovaries ached.

"What's that a map of?" he asked while decimating half of the chicken sub she had brought back for him. April had needed to do a few chores at lunchtime, and she had stopped in to see her mother. Mama had been frying up some chicken cutlets and sent her back to the office with a sandwich that could feed three people instead of two.

While she chewed, April looked over her shoulder where she had hung up a map of her dream cruise vacation. Swallowing, she touched the poster affectionately. "I'm planning to take a transatlantic cruise next year." She traced the path with her finger. "There and back. It'll take twenty-five days and I'm going to see eleven countries."

"Have you ever been overseas before?" he asked.

"Nope," she admitted. "It'll be the first time." Sometimes it felt like her whole life had been on hold—and this cruise would be the starting point. It would be the ultimate pinnacle of her evolution. She'd be out of her comfort zone on so many levels. If she could handle this, she knew she could handle anything that life threw at her. She didn't have to always play it safe. And this life-changing trip would convince her that it was okay to take risks now and then.

Unless, of course, the boat sank or something.

No. No. She wasn't going to think like that. There were plenty of lifeboats anyway. And hardly an iceberg in sight. She hoped. Nibbling on her lower lip, she resisted the urge to see if her boat would be sailing the same waters the *Titanic* had been in.

On this trip, she was going to dance, drink, gamble, and shop until she fell into bed exhausted every night, only to do it all over again the next day in a different country. She was going to take her planners and lists though. She couldn't quite go cold turkey yet, but she was getting better.

"Why do you want to go?"

"Why not?" she said, not understanding his question.

"Why there, instead of Disney World or Key West?"

"I want to see the world. I want to visit places that I've only read about in books. I want to touch history." April realized she was about to start waxing poetic and reined herself back in. "I want to experience new ideas and cultures. Even if it's only for a month." She touched the map again. "I want the unexpected."

He was quiet for so long, she began to get uncomfortable. "What?"

"Nothing. I think it's great. You're whole face lights up. Who are you going with?"

"No one." That was the beauty of it. For the first time in her life, she would be too far away to drop everything and ride to the rescue. Her sisters and mother would manage without her. She had prepared them for this. Aside from her mom's little setback with Stuart, April was sure that they would do just fine for a month. And then maybe a month would become two and on and on until a year went by.

And maybe she would finally be able to turn over their finances to them. And they would be ready to take control...

It was a dream. But it was her dream.

"You can't go alone," he sputtered.

"Why not?"

"It's not safe."

"Of course, it is." Although April had to admit that she was a bit unnerved traveling so far by herself, she was excited, too. "I'll be on a boat with five thousand other people."

"All of them strangers."

"You sound like my mother." April wasn't even going to think about the reality of being alone until a month before the cruise. She'd even already scheduled in a freak-out about it in her planner to take some of the seriousness out of it. It was silly, but it helped her stay focused. She couldn't worry about any reservations she had about it now, but she had allotted time for it.

Cole just grunted in response. She thought that had ended that discussion, but after he came back in from one of his classes, he picked up the conversation as if no time had passed.

"Why a month-long cruise?" he asked, hitching his hip on the desk while he glared at the poster.

"Oh let me see... Gourmet food every night, entertainment, shopping, gambling... And more importantly, seeing all those different countries. An itinerary like the one I've planned takes some time."

"Gambling?" he said.

"That's what got your attention?"

"You play the slot machines, don't you?"

April tapped her pencil on the desk as she looked up at him. He was wearing soft blue jeans faded almost to the color of his eyes. "If they look like fun."

"Ever play poker?"

She shook her head.

"Any time you want some lessons, let me know."

April had a sudden flash of sitting across from him in her

bra and panties while they played strip poker.

"Do I even want to know why you're blushing like that?" he asked.

"I'm not blushing. It's just a little hot in here. I think I'm going to go out and get some fresh air." She was painfully aware that he intended to follow her outside and she resisted the urge to fan herself.

Trent and Billy were setting up the chute for the adult cowboys looking to practice on Red.

"You ever ride a real bull?" she asked him, leaning against the fence.

"Yeah, I've been on Red. He tossed me on my ass in a lot less than eight seconds."

"Did you get hurt?"

"Nah, he's not a vindictive bull and I landed well."

Once the student had his seat, Billy opened up the chute and Red came out, twirling and jumping. Trent and Billy shouted directions to the cowboy, but he lost his grip and hit the ground. Billy jogged over to get the student out of the way, but now that the cowboy was no longer on his back Red wasn't interested in him. Instead, he ambled away from the commotion, snorting in disgust.

"It's a lot cuter when the kids are on the sheep," Cole said.

"I can't wait to see that."

"I've got to get the horses ready for the middle-school kids. Do you want to help?"

April really didn't, but she also wanted to get some exercise and fresh air into her day. Trent's records were going to keep her inside for a long time. "Sure. But I've got to warn you, horses and I have a mutual hate-hate relationship."

"Not these horses. They're the gentle ones that the kids practice with."

"All right," April said. She didn't say that it didn't matter to her, that she thought all horses were monsters. Then he'd think she was a huge chicken.

"Besides—" Cole reached down and grabbed her hand. "I only have to behave myself when we're at our desks, right?"

She giggled and linked her fingers through his. "I thought you had lost interest."

"No." Cole rubbed his thumb over her wrist. "I've just been working nonstop. We're still on for our date after the picnic tomorrow right?"

"Of course. I've been looking forward to it."

"I've got to go to my second job around eight, but that should give us a few hours to get reacquainted," he said.

"I can't wait," she said. And she couldn't. Being with him all day, but not able to touch him, had her about to jump out of her skin.

Cole led her into the horse barn, where there were ten of the dreadful beasts glaring down at her. She was prepared to glare back when Cole pulled her into his arms. "I've been wanting to kiss you all week. Here's your chance to say no."

"Not on your life." April wrapped her arms around his neck and pressed her lips to his. Wild April Grayson was kissing a man in a barn when she should be behind her desk working. She'd make it up to Trent. But for right now, she was reliving how good it felt to be a little naughty. She had been slipping back into her Old April ways. It was time to get back on the Wild April train.

Damn, she had thought she had imagined how good his kisses made her feel. They even made her temporarily forget about the ten demon spawns behind her. Cole's mouth was persuasive, and she opened up to him so their tongues could play. She pressed against him and his back hit the barn wall with a thump. Deepening the kiss, Cole gripped her ass with both hands and held her against his hardness.

"I don't think I can wait until tomorrow night," she gasped when he went for the curve of her neck.

"Too bad," Cole grunted. "We're doing it in a bed this time."

"That hay bale looks kind of cozy," she said, only half joking.

With a groan, he held her away from him. "You're an evil temptress."

Yes!

April resisted doing a fist bump. No one had ever called her that before. Evil temptress was definitely Wild April territory.

He gave her one last fierce kiss before going to tend to the horses. She was still riding the high from the sexy tingles going through her body that she barely noticed when Cole brought one of the horses out of his stall and put a halter on it.

"Lead him out to the back pasture and open the gate for me, will you?" Cole held out the lead rope.

"Me?" April backed away with her hands up and plastered herself against the wall when the animal snorted and tossed his head. "Uh-uh, no way. He'll take off on me."

"Just stay on his left side and keep a firm hand on the rope."

"I'm sorry, Cole. I can't." April backed slowly away from the horse, ready to dodge behind the door if the beast lunged at her.

"Bathsheba isn't like your sisters' horses."

"That's what they all say." April cleared the barn and took off running back to the school. But when she got back to their office, she started to feel foolish. She probably could have led Bathsheba to the pen, but she just lost it around horses. Hell, her hands were *still* shaking.

She sat back down and went to work. After a while, her pulse returned to normal and the shame of her cowardly behavior faded. When she finally took her a break, she texted her sisters. The horse incident had made her think of them, and she'd realized how much she missed them. They hadn't had a lot of time to chat lately. Merry had forwarded some pictures of a baby llama that had just been born and June had sent a picture of something called trash can nachos. The dish looked appalling and delicious at the same time.

Too soon, it was time to get back to work. She was actually making headway when Cole came back from his afternoon classes.

"Why a whole month? Why not a week or two weeks? You could see a lot of places in two weeks," Cole said, launching himself into his chair and kicking his feet up on his desk.

It took a minute for April to come out of the comforting world of sums and figure out what the heck he was talking about. "Oh, the cruise." She supposed that was better than trying to defend her irrational fear of horses after all these years, but not as entertaining as exploring where that kiss might lead to tomorrow night. Tossing her pencil on the desk, she blew out a sigh. "Most people can't take off a month from work to go on a cruise. When I got laid off, I was devastated."

"I'm sorry," he said.

"I did nothing wrong. Ever." April gave a half laugh. "For five years, I came to work a half hour early. Most days I worked through my lunch hour and I was the last to leave the office at the end of the day. I never took any time off unless I was truly sick. I was a devoted worker. And where did that get me?"

"Nowhere?" Cole ventured a guess.

"You got it. I felt so betrayed, so stupid for giving that job everything. Every sacrifice I made for my career seemed foolish. And I wanted to find a bright side." April looked back at the map. "I've always wanted to travel out of the country, but there never seemed to be enough time. Now I had it. So, I booked the cruise." She turned back to him defiantly. "It was the best thing I'd ever done for myself."

"Good for you."

"I've always been the responsible one in my family. The one who could be counted on, just like at work. And like my job, where did that get me?"

"I'm sure your sisters appreciated you."

"Sometimes yes, sometimes no." April snorted. "I decided I'd try to live my life a little like they lived theirs. I wanted to be Wild April Grayson, and have old biddies shake their heads at me and say, 'She's just like her sisters.'"

"Are you planning on riding your horse down Main Street buck naked?"

"I hate horses," April said.

"Any other naked activities planned?"

"Aside from tomorrow night?" she teased.

"Yeah."

"As many as I can get."

"How the hell am I going to teach three classes and then go work in the fields tonight with that on my mind?" Cole groaned.

"You asked." She shrugged.

"I'm glad we're getting a chance at another round. I'm looking forward to taking my time."

"Me too." April's heart thumped a bit faster.

"I wish I was boyfriend material, though."

"What do you mean?"

He sighed and gave her such a forlorn look, she began to feel uncomfortable.

"I don't want to take advantage of your sweet and sexy nature, so I've got to be honest here. You're the hottest thing I've ever set eyes on, but I don't have time to be a good boyfriend. I work nonstop, day and night, and when I'm not working, I'm helping my parents." He leaned back in his chair again. "I'd totally understand if you want to change your mind about tomorrow."

April shook her head. "I don't understand."

"You deserve a guy who will put you first in his life. You know, take you out to dinner and dates. Buy you fancy things. Spend time with you. There's not enough time in the day for me to do that." He rubbed his temples. "I wish it were different, but my parents have some hefty hospital bills that never seem to stop arriving."

"Trent had mentioned to me that your parents were ill. How are they doing?"

"Getting better every day, but it's slow going. Just when we pay one bill off, another pops up. The insurance was taking some of the heat off, but now, with pre-existing conditions and out-of-plan expenses..." Cole grimaced. "Look, I don't mean to complain. I just didn't want you to think I was avoiding you or making excuses. Let's just say, I wish we met five years ago."

"Five years ago, I don't think I would have had sex with you in your truck."

"That's okay," Cole said. "I'd have been lucky to even get a kiss ten years ago."

She hated to admit it, but he was right. But she'd changed. And he'd soon find out just how much. But for now, she'd let it rest. "I hear what you're saying. I know what it's like to have your family depend on you. I didn't let Merry and June out on the road alone for five years after high school. It was hard to cut the cord, but we're all better for it. Not that I'm saying you should stop helping your parents..." April rushed to add.

"I almost lost them, and things will never be back to normal. They haven't realized that though, so it makes it harder."

April nodded. "My mother is stubborn, too. She's a hairdresser and refuses to cut down on her hours to save her feet and back. She loves the hustle and bustle of the salon. When we were on the road, she was very popular with the cowgirls. She's a wizard with a flat iron."

"I'm going to assume that's not the same flatiron that brands cattle."

"You'd be correct." She liked the easy teasing they had. "What do your parents do?"

"My mother used to run a foundation for underprivileged children, but after her gall bladder surgery, she stepped down and consults when she feels up to it. My dad was a rancher before he retired and sold off the herd and pastures. Before his illness, he was driving Mom crazy, digging up her gardens and fixing things around the house, whether they needed to be fixed or not. But these days, they're both too tired to do much of anything. My father's chemo and radiation schedule takes a lot out of both of them."

"I'm so sorry. It must be tough on you. Are you the only child?"

"Yes, but I have help. A home health aide comes in to help them when I'm not around, for a few hours at least. Gwen is awesome. She loves them and they love her. Sooner or later, I'm going to have to hire someone else for overnight, but hopefully, not for a while yet." He still had a bleak look on his face. "Sometimes it feels like I'm at the bottom of a very deep well and every time I start to make some progress in climbing out, I lose my hand holds and go sliding back down again."

"You'll get there. You work too hard not to."

"I wish I could spend more time with you," he said again, and the truth in his voice made her throat tighten.

"We're spending time together now."

"We're supposed to be working," he said with a self-depreciating grin.

"I'm okay with mixing business with pleasure. And as long as we get our jobs done, Trent shouldn't have a problem with it."

"But are *you* okay with that?"

"I'm okay with casual."

Except Cole didn't make what they had feel casual. That was part of his allure. And there was no way she was going to run away from that.

"You're too good to be true."

"Not anymore, I'm not. I'm one of the bad girls your mama warned you about."

"One of those wild Grayson sisters."

"Absolutely."

Cole got up from his seat and stretched. The hem of his T-shirt rode up and she got a tantalizing hint of his abs. "I've got to get the kids on the horses. Don't work too late."

"I've got a system now." She pointed to the neat piles that finally made sense to her.

"I'm glad you see it. It still looks like a big old mess to me."

It was, but she would get it in order. She just needed to do it year by year, until it all fell in line. "It'll all work out."

Cole paused in the doorway. "I know it's not any of my business, but is Trent getting a lot of money back?"

"I really can't tell you," she said apologetically.

"Actually, I didn't mean it like that. I don't care about Trent's refund. I meant, can you squeeze more money out of the government, in most cases?"

She smirked. "It depends. But I know what a person can deduct legally, and all my clients know I will point out the best ways to save and take advantage of opportunities."

"Maybe I'll hire you to take a look at my parents' taxes after this."

Oh no. She was sliding into being Accountant April in his eyes. And yet, it sounded like she could help, so how could she refuse? "I bet we'll find that more than a few of those medical bills could be deductible."

Some of the tension eased from Cole's shoulders. "We'll talk more later."

April wanted to do more than talk, but she was willing to bide her time. "Be careful around those creatures."

"The kids?" Cole looked puzzled.

"The horses." She shuddered.

"We're going to talk about that, too," he said and then left to teach his class.

After trying to get back into the groove of working with Trent's taxes—and failing—April got up to pour herself some of the sweet tea that Kelly had dropped off this morning, and pondered her situation. She didn't want to be an accountant booty call for Cole, but she also didn't want to give him up. Not just yet. Still, she wished she could be as cavalier about men as her sisters were. They didn't let anyone get close enough to matter. But no matter how much she wished otherwise, April wasn't like them. And she knew she was going to have to work extra hard to make sure Cole didn't worm his way into her heart.

Chapter Nine

COLE WORKED ALL morning at his parents' house, getting the first level in order. He had just tiled the bathroom and once it was dry, he would rehang the door. That would finish the renovations. Or at least he hoped it would.

"Is there anything you need from me before I go?" he asked his mom.

"Just take over my fruit salad and a basket of biscuits for the Sullivans' barbecue."

"Thanks."

"I didn't want you to go over there empty-handed."

"I was going to stop at the store," he protested.

"Well, now you don't have to."

"I hope you saved some of those biscuits for me," his dad said as he came into the room, walking shakily on his cane.

"Dad, you should really use the walker," Cole said, exchanging a look with Gwen who was standing right next to his father just in case the cane didn't support him.

His father made a disgusted sound and slowly sat down at the kitchen table.

"I've got this," Gwen said.

"Thanks." Cole knew his parents were in good hands, so he gathered up the biscuits and fruit salad and headed out to his truck. Normally he would have tried to blow off the Sullivans' barbecue, but Trent had said there was going to be an important announcement and he shouldn't miss it.

Besides, it let him take April out on a date. He was looking forward to spending a few hours with her, even if he couldn't stay the night. Kyle Mantooth needed a few night riders to look out for his herd and Cole didn't sleep much these days anyway. Every time he closed his eyes, he couldn't get that failed high-stakes poker game out of his mind. Maybe he should go to Vegas, get a big score, and take it easy for a while. Or at least until the next month of bills came in.

"Hey there, Cole," Emily greeted him when he walked up to the picnic tables to drop off his mother's goodies. She was slowly taking over the day-to-day running of the ranch.

"Have you seen April?"

"Not yet, but she said she was going to be here. How do you like working with her? I bet she's so quiet, you don't even know she's there."

"Not exactly," Cole said, but he didn't want to explain to his boss's sister-in-law that he had the hots for the new accountant.

"Oh, I almost forgot. Donovan wanted me to send you his way when you got here. I think he's still in his clubhouse. Flush him out for me, will you?"

"You got it." Cole had intended to stick close to the farmhouse until April got there, but it seemed like she knew

Emily through her sister, so maybe she'd feel comfortable talking with the family until he got back. He wouldn't be too long. He had an idea of what Donovan wanted to talk to him about and he wasn't really interested.

He walked down to the clubhouse instead of taking the Gator because he was going to be on a horse all night and he could use the extra exercise. Donovan Link was a professional hunter, but when he wasn't thinning out the feral hog herds around the Three Sisters Ranch, he booked safari-like tours for city folk who wanted to see some wildlife. Rumor had it there was a white elk named Ghost wandering around the property, but Cole hadn't seen it yet.

When he came up on the clubhouse, Donovan was playing cards with ranch foreman Nate Pierson, Esteban Lopez—Nate's second in command—and a couple of ranch hands Cole didn't know.

"Beer?" Donovan asked, gesturing to the ice chest next to him.

"Don't mind if I do." As he reached into the cooler, he noticed they were playing Omaha.

"Want to be dealt in?" Donovan asked.

"PLO or fixed limit?" Cole asked. Pot limit could get expensive, but fixed limit kept more people from folding.

"No limit."

Yee hah! Maybe he'd triple his money. That would be worth the time he spent here. Cole never used to put a dollar amount on his time...until he had to start making choices that depended on getting the most bang for his buck. Hauling hay for fifteen dollars an hour or riding a horse all night long for thirty dollars an hour was a no-brainer. Instead of just having fun at a picnic, Cole had figured to network a bit until April showed up. Now, he could add a little profit to his day. Maybe he'd even win a little spending cash to take April out to dinner or something—if they could manage to fit it into his schedule.

"Why not?" He exchanged a hundred-dollar bill for some chips and sat down to play. "Emily's looking for you," he told Donovan.

Esteban dealt the cards for the round.

Cole peeked at his four cards. When it was his turn to bet, he called the big blind like everyone else. Why not? It was only two bucks to see the flop.

Donovan glanced at his watch. "We've got some time. I told her we'd be wrapping up here around two. She's just champing at the bit because she wants to make an announcement to everyone."

"Everyone's not here yet," Nate said.

Esteban dealt three flop cards. One was a king and one a nine. The third card didn't help Cole at all, but he was looking at two pair.

Everyone checked, which meant unfortunately no money went into the pot. Cole had a sneaking suspicion that if the rest of the game went like this, he wasn't going to do more than break even.

Esteban dealt the next card.

"So what's the big announcement?" one of the ranch hands asked, checking the bet.

"Emily and I set the wedding date for June." Donovan

bet two dollars.

"About time," Nate grumbled, calling the bet. Cole wasn't sure if he was talking about the bet or Donovan's announcement.

"I fold." One of the ranch hands tossed his cards down and went for another beer.

Cole called as well. He knew he really should have folded but what was that Wayne Gretzky quote? You miss one hundred percent of the shots you don't take?

The other two ranch hands folded, but Esteban stayed in.

"Three weddings in one year would have been too much," Donovan said, referring to Trent and Kelly's June wedding last year, as well as Nate and Janice's wedding on Christmas Eve. "Besides, it was touch and go there for a while with Frank's health."

"I thought he was taking it easy," Cole said, watching as Esteban burned a card and prepared to turn over the last community card.

Everyone at the table laughed.

"That'll be the day," Nate said.

"Sarah would have to chain him to the bed or something," Esteban said, flipping over the ace of hearts.

Shit. Now everyone had a pair of aces and likely Donovan had a trip, if not a full house himself. That left Cole with a pair of kings and a pair of aces, which normally was a great hand. Just not in this case.

"And dollars to doughnuts, he'd be out working on the trail with a sawed-off bedpost, barking orders as usual,"

Donovan replied, opening the bet with four dollars.

Nate glared at him and raised another four.

With the bet at eight dollars, Cole threw in his cards and so did Esteban.

After a minor bidding war between the two brothers-in-law, Donovan cheerfully showed a full house, aces over nines. Nate cracked a rare smirk and revealed a full house of his own. Aces full of kings.

"Fuck," Donovan said.

They set up for the next hand, Donovan made the pitch that Cole had been waiting for. "So, this is fun, right?"

"Hell of a lot of fun," Nate chimed in.

Donovan rolled his eyes. "What do you say about running a poker game for my hunting lodge every Friday night that I've got a party? Interested?"

"Isn't that illegal?" Esteban asked, scowling at his cards before tossing them away before seeing the flop.

"Only if the house takes a cut," Cole said, betting three dollars. He had a much better hand this time. Cole had figured that Donovan was going to ask him to be the dealer for his clients. Donovan had been hinting around the fact that he knew a lot of hunters who would love to play poker on their weekend retreats.

"He's charging them to hunt or go on a safari, not to play poker," Nate said, raising the bet.

Nate was on fire today, but Cole knew he had a habit of being an aggressive player. Cole called.

"Right, which means I can't play because that's a gray area. But the rest of you could." Donovan looked like he was going to call, but then folded. "And we can bill it as 'Try your luck against a former World Series Poker player.' I bet a lot of people would come just for that alone."

"Wait, do you want me to deal or do you want me to play?" Dealing the cards all night wouldn't add up, even if he counted on the tips the players gave him. He'd be better off night riding or hauling hay. But if he was playing alongside the players, that could turn a better profit for him.

"Play, of course."

"Isn't it going to piss off your clients if I take them for a couple of hundred dollars each?"

"If you win," Nate snorted and raised.

Cole called.

"No, my clients may be mostly good old boys, but they'd respect a clean game. And you could sweeten the loss by giving a few tips on how they could improve."

"What about security?" Cole said, an idea coming to him. "What if someone finds out about the game and tries to rob it?"

"We all carry rifles," Donovan deadpanned.

"And this is private property," Nate said. "It's hard to sneak all the way down here without someone noticing."

This could make up for the high-stakes game he'd lost. One big win and he could pay Gwen's salary for the next year. He'd have to get Vic in touch with Donovan. Some of the regular players would likely only be interested in the game, but there might be others who wouldn't mind a weekend getaway with a Friday and Saturday night game.

"I'm all in," he said to both Donovan and Nate.

Pushing in his stack of chips, he waited for Nate to fold or call. He read Nate right and Nate matched his bet.

Cole's flush beat Nate's straight.

"Damn it." Nate thumped his fist on the table.

Donovan reached over and shook Cole's hand.

Chapter Ten

A PRIL PUSHED DOWN the slight discomfort she felt as she got out of her car, balancing her pot of brown sugar baked beans that had been simmering since last night in the slow cooker. She made sure they were vegetarian because she knew Emily would appreciate another dish she could eat. Emily was one of the few people she knew here at the picnic, although she recognized a bunch of ranch hands as well.

June would be right at home here. She and Emily had been inseparable before life took them in different directions. April had been surprised to hear that Emily had come back to Last Stand, Texas. She'd figured Emily would continue to travel the world with the Peace Corps. But when their father's health had become an issue, Emily had returned to the ranch, along with her sisters.

As April walked over to the buffet table, she caught sight of Frank Sullivan, the patriarch of the family. He walked with a cane, but it slowed him down as much as you would expect a stubborn old Texan man to be slowed down by something as trivial as two major heart attacks.

"Hi, Mrs. Sullivan," April said, as Frank's wife came to help her with the pot of beans.

"You're not a little girl anymore. You can call me Sarah."

Yeah, and that would be as easy as Kelly calling April's mother Penny.

"Did you know I'm working for Trent now?"

"Yes, Kelly mentioned he had brought you on to help him with his books. Maybe when you finish his, we could get you to look at our taxes, too."

"I'd be happy to," April said. It was as she thought. It didn't look like she'd have any trouble building her client list just through word of mouth. "Is Kelly around?" April hadn't seen her yet.

"She's still a little under the weather, but I'm hoping she'll make an appearance."

"I brought her some tea and biscuits. They're in the car."

"She'll be happy to hear that. Sometimes that's all she can eat in a day." Sarah frowned. "I'm worried about her."

"What did the doctor say?"

"That the baby is healthy and Kelly is healthy. He said the sickness should go away soon, but he's been saying that for months now." She shook her head and turned back to the table of food she was getting ready.

Before April could offer to help, Emily came up to her and gave April a hug. "I'm so happy to see you."

April was a little taken aback, because she and Emily didn't usually hug when they saw each other, but she hugged her back, missing her own little sister.

"You must be so worried about June. I know I am."

"Uh, well no more than usual."

"I can't picture her in rehab. She's going to be climbing

the walls."

"What?" April froze.

"Emily!" Sarah turned around to glare at her daughter.

Emily covered her mouth with both hands. "Oh my gosh, I'm so sorry. I thought you knew."

April shook her head. "I haven't spoken to June in a few weeks, but I texted her the other day. What happened?"

"I shouldn't…" Emily said, looking stricken.

"Go on now," Sarah said. "You've come this far."

"Right." Emily put her arm around April and guided her away from the crowd of people by the house. "I'm so sorry I put my foot in it."

"That's okay," April said. "I'm sure you didn't realize that June hadn't told me."

"She said she was going to." Emily opened the screen door and April followed her inside. "We can talk in the kitchen. That'll give us some privacy."

"Thanks."

April pulled out her phone and looked at it. There weren't any missed calls from either of her sisters or her mother. She sat down at the kitchen table while Emily paced.

"I'm not sure if June told you, but Donovan and I are engaged."

April nodded. She vaguely remembered that June was looking forward to being a bridesmaid, but the wedding had been put off for some reason.

"Last year was crazy, so Donovan and I decided to wait until this year to get married." Emily leaned in conspiratorially. "That's the real reason for the picnic. We're going to announce the date today."

"Congratulations," April said through numbed lips. She wished Emily would get to the point.

"Anyway," Emily said, pausing for a shaky breath. "Since June is in Galveston right now..."

That was news to her, too, but April didn't keep track of her sisters' rodeo schedules unless it was a major one. She knew that they were headed to Vegas at the end of this month, but that was because they'd been looking forward to it all year.

"I was hoping she could drop by the picnic so I could get a picture with all my bridesmaids and maybe hang out for a few hours. But when I called her, she was just going into the facility."

"What facility?"

"The Galveston Center. Apparently, it was court-ordered."

April held a hand over the pain in her stomach. "She was arrested?"

"I'm not sure. She glossed over the facts. Said she blacked out and woke up in a jail cell. It scared the crap out of her."

"I bet," April said, worried for her baby sister. June had always been a hard drinker, but even April had noticed that it had gotten worse lately.

"Merry headed down to help her, but long story short, June has to stay there for ninety days."

"I'm glad Merry is with her." April was going to knock their heads together, though, for not telling her about this.

"June seemed to be in good spirits," Emily said consolingly. "I told her to give me a call when she could, but she's not allowed outside calls for two weeks."

April grimaced. "Maybe I should go out there."

Emily shook her head. "No visitors, either."

"Wow." April put her face in her hands. "She's really done it this time."

"I'm sorry you had to hear it from me."

Taking a deep breath, April straightened up. "No, I'm glad you told me. Thank you. I'm sorry if this puts a damper on your party."

"It does and it doesn't. At least June will be out in time for my wedding."

"If she behaves herself," April said darkly, standing up. "I should let you get back to the party."

"I know this was a surprise to you. Feel free to stay inside for a few moments, while you let it all sink in." Emily gave her another quick hug and then left.

April walked around the kitchen, not wanting to believe what she'd just heard. So she immediately called Merry. "Does Mama know?" April said as soon as her sister answered.

"Know what?" Merry hedged.

"That June got arrested and put in a rehab facility for the next ninety days."

Merry groaned. "Emily told you?"

"She thought I already knew. I'm working with Trent on her ranch now. Why didn't you guys call me?"

"Because we had it handled. We didn't want to worry

anyone." She sighed. "Honestly, we were going to come clean to you and Mama in a couple of weeks, once June can take phone calls and have visitors."

"Is she all right?" April asked, hanging on to the door-frame for support.

"She will be. I think things are going to get better for her from here on in."

"Does she need anything? Surely, the facility will allow packages."

"I think she's good. It's just going to be rough paying the bills without insurance."

April wanted to bang her head against the wall. They had come so far. "Can she go on a payment plan?"

"I think so. At least, that's what the admins said. But you know June. She wants to pay it out of the retirement fund you set up for her."

"Absolutely not," April said. "The withdrawal fees will kill her. Let the money stay where it is. If she's that worried about it, I can help."

"Help how? You just got fired from your job."

"I got laid off," April said crisply. "But I've got money in my cruise fund and some savings as well."

"No, don't touch that. You've been jabbering nonstop about this world cruise for the past year. There's no way June would want to take that away from you. It would kill her more than the withdrawal fees."

"So what are we going to do?" April asked.

"I guess I'm not going to retire just yet. There are a couple of lucrative purses coming up that I can shoot for. The

NFR is back on the schedule. I'm going to go in for roping and barrel racing."

The National Finals Rodeo paid out the best, but it was tough to get into. A rider had to be in the top fifteen contestants in qualifying rodeos. Merry was in the top ten, but she hadn't intended on going this year.

"Can you still get in?"

"I'll be taking June's place."

June would be pissed, but it wasn't like she could break out of rehab to ride. Merry didn't sound too thrilled about it either. June might be the better roper, but Merry was the better barrel racer. Still, April knew that she wanted to be out of the saddle and behind the announcer's table.

"I agreed to wear her sponsorship patches in addition to my own. I'm going to look like a billboard," Merry said.

"That's not fair to you."

"What do you want me to do? She's my sister."

"Our sister. I want to help, too."

Merry sighed. "I figured. But this is June's mess. We can't do everything for her."

"We're not. We're just here to support her."

"But whatever you do, don't tell Mama. June will do that in a couple of weeks. If she asks you if you've heard from June, just say no."

"It wouldn't be a lie," April grumbled.

"I've got to go. I've got to find a way to board Athena, so Mama doesn't find out about it. Do you think Emily's got room there?"

"I don't know." April made a face. Athena was June's

mare. June had wanted to name her after the Greek goddess of wisdom. But April never forgot that Athena was Ares's sister—and had a similar temperament. After April's accident, Ares had gone to another owner—one who could handle him. Athena, however, had stayed with June.

"If Emily is taking boarders, I can send Athena this week. And I'd really appreciate it if you could just keep an eye on her…"

"Me?" April interrupted. "That horse hates me, and the feeling is mutual."

"April, you said you wanted to help."

"Fine. I'll make sure she doesn't kill anyone."

"Thanks. I'll call Emily right now."

"All right. Keep me in the loop about June."

"I will."

April put her phone away and tried to get into the spirit of the picnic. This was a special day for Emily and Donovan, and she was looking forward to seeing Cole outside of work and being alone with him a little later.

That thought cheered her up a bit and she went back outside to join the party, hoping Kelly would show up. She'd love to have a long chat with her friend.

Sarah caught up to her and handed her a cold glass of lemonade.

"Thanks." April took a grateful sip. It was perfect—not too sweet, and not too sour.

"Everything all right?" she asked.

"It will be." April had to trust that June could take care of herself. She couldn't allow herself to feel guilty or backslide into being a mother hen. June was responsible for her own actions and April had a new business to concentrate on…as well as a cruise to look forward to next year.

"Everyone here loves to watch your sisters compete when we're lucky to get the events televised. They're great athletes."

"Yes, they are." April tensed up, expecting the inevitable question—the one that always came up whenever her sisters were mentioned.

"So how come you never went out on the rodeo circuit?"

There it was. "I wasn't much of one for horses. I preferred books."

Like everyone she'd ever met did when they heard her answer, Sarah looked at April as if she was an interesting new species of butterfly. It was like they heard the words "I don't like horses," but they didn't quite understand what they meant.

"Well, I'm sure Janice could help you work out your problem with horses. She's got two beautiful purebreds. One is a thoroughbred that used to race down in Kentucky where she used to work."

Janice was currently laughing with her husband, Nate, who was trying to herd a bunch of dogs into a large pen so they would stop begging for food. He wound up picking up a beagle and a Chihuahua mix under each arm and physically carrying them into the containment area. Unfortunately, the large husky mix wasn't going to be that easy.

"Synergy could have been a Derby contender, but he didn't have the discipline. But he has the speed. You should see him go."

April didn't quite know how to tell Sarah that those high-strung racehorses were just as terrifying to her as her mother's pony, Tulip. She couldn't imagine relating to something three times Tulip's size because it probably had three times the pony's attitude.

Cole and a bunch of men caught her eye as they drove in, packed to maximum capacity on one Gator. She was surprised the little ATV didn't tip over from the extra weight.

"Those boys," Sarah said, exasperated.

"Grandma, can you open this?" Kelly's daughter, Alissa, came over, holding up a bottle of root beer.

"I sure can. April, can you excuse me?"

"Of course." April was glad for the interruption because it gave her an excuse to make her way closer to Cole. She saw that he had picked her out almost immediately and it was almost comical how they both wound their way around the people at the party to get to each other.

"Hi," she said, uncaring that she sounded a little breathless.

"I've been waiting for you to get here," Cole said.

"Well, here I am."

They stood awkwardly grinning at each other for a moment. "Do you want to grab a plate of food and see if we can get a table for two?" she asked.

"I doubt there's much room for privacy with all these people around, but Sarah's buttermilk fried chicken is calling my name."

April almost reached for his hand, but stopped herself just in time. They weren't an item. She didn't want to fuel any gossip that there was an office romance brewing. She didn't want to embarrass him, but she *was* hoping that they could be more than a brief fling. She understood about him not having a lot of time for dating, but she wasn't a teenager who needed attention twenty-four, seven. She was much more into quality than quantity.

As they filled up their plates, April told him about her sister June.

"I'm sorry to hear about that, but June strikes me as a fighter. If she wants to kick the habit, she will."

"I know. I just wish I could make things easier for her."

Cole reached across the table and gave her hand a squeeze. "You've helped them with their dreams. Now, it's time for yours."

It felt like Tulip, that damned pony of her mother's, had kicked her in the chest. No one had ever said something like that to her before. She had to take a moment to relish the thought.

"You look tired," she said. "Haven't you been sleeping?"

He gave a half shrug. "I've been busy, trying to keep the bill collectors at bay."

"Do you need any help? I know a few people who are really good with investments."

"At some point. Right now, I need to figure out how to manage for the next few months rather than the next few years."

April understood where he was coming from. While she

was doing both Trent's personal and business taxes, maybe she could come across a way that both he and his employees could win if she found an investment that worked for all of them.

"You don't want to work so hard that you get sick," she said instead.

"I'm okay. I take breaks when I can, and I'll sleep when I'm dead."

She cringed. "Don't say things like that."

"It's just a saying. I've got to be at the Mantooth ranch around eight. I'm going to be watching the cattle overnight until about three thirty a.m."

"You're going to be in the saddle all night long and go to work tomorrow?" April thought he was crazy.

"Luckily, I don't work tomorrow until noon, so I can catch up on some sleep."

"Are you sure you don't just want to take a nap before heading over?"

"I'll be fine," Cole assured her. "I wouldn't miss this chance to be with you."

"Where are you working tomorrow?" She wished he'd take some time for himself.

"I'll be helping with the chores at the Braxton farm. They need someone on the tractor and the hay baler and I'm handy with both. It's good money." He shrugged. "What are your plans for Sunday?"

"My mother's cooking a big meal after church, and if I don't show up I'm in hot water, even though I'd rather spend it binge-watching some new series. Cheddar and I have just discovered *Lucifer* and we're plowing through five seasons."

"Cheddar?"

"My cat. He likes to hog the blankets."

"I can't remember the last time I watched something that wasn't on ESPN. Nothing holds my interest. I wind up falling asleep."

"That's your body trying to tell you something." April poked him in the arm.

"Can I get everybody's attention, please?" Emily stood up, with her arm around Donovan. "We've got some special news for you." Emily was radiant as she looked out over the crowd. "As you all know, last year was so crazy. Small disasters kept popping up, one after the other, so Donovan and I had decided to put off our wedding. Well, I'm happy to announce that we've re-set the date. We'll be getting married here on the ranch in June, and you're all invited. But most importantly…" She grinned and met everyone's eyes. "You're also all invited to the bachelor and bachelorette parties."

Janice stood up. The last remaining dogs to be corralled circled around her, barking in excitement. "And believe me, they're going to be wild."

There was that word again. April shimmied with happiness in her seat. It was all starting to come together for her.

Chapter Eleven

WHILE APRIL WAS chatting with the Sullivan sisters, Cole snuck away to make a phone call to Vic.

"I'm going to make your day," Cole said when Vic picked up. "Hell, I may make your entire month."

"I could use some good news," Vic said.

"Donovan Link at the Hunters' Club at the Three Sisters Ranch is looking to host poker nights for groups who book his package tours."

"What type of tours?"

"In season, hunting tours. Only for population control and mostly feral hogs."

"Those damn things breed like rabbits."

"The rest of the time, he's got weekends available for trail rides, nature safaris…"

"Safaris? This is South Texas, not South Africa."

"From what I understand, it's a cool tour, filled with all sorts of Texas wildlife."

Vic snorted. "If I want to see that, I'll look out my back door."

"Anyway," Cole said. "Do you think your whales would be interested in a weekend at the Hunters' Club?" The whales were gamblers who habitually spent a large amount in casinos and private games. If they were in Vegas, the casino would comp them a room and all the buffets they could eat. Unfortunately, the entry fee that Vic charged wouldn't cover that. It was going to take a lot of fast talk to get the whales to pay for a weekend out of their own pocket. Still, Donovan had a sterling reputation for his hunting tours and Vic knew how to spin things.

"Maybe. How much is it?"

"Work that out with Donovan and save me a seat at the table."

"I'll see what I can do. In the meantime, keep next Friday or Saturday free. I'm working on setting something up at the Bluebonnet Country Club in San Antonio. It might be for members only though. If it is, I'll put in a good word for you and see if I can get you a guest pass. I can't promise anything, though."

Cole swore under his breath. He could keep those dates open, but if Vic couldn't get him into the game, then he'd be out the couple hundred bucks it would take to get his foot in the door. Cole would have to think of it the same way he would if he'd been at the table. He'd be gambling $300, hoping the risk would pan out to $30,000. And if it didn't turn out so well, he could spend some more time with April, helping her work on her wild side. That sounded like a win all the way around.

Everyone was having a good time at the picnic, eating until they were stuffed and then playing lawn games like bocce and horseshoes. Frank was getting pretty competitive with Billy, and everyone was egging on the good-natured rivalry.

Cole mingled as much as he had the patience for. He tried to be discreet when he checked his watch, but exactly forty-five minutes after Emily and Donovan made their announcement, he tapped April on her shoulder.

"Let's go," he whispered in her ear and was delighted when she shivered in reaction.

He waited patiently while she disengaged from the conversation she was having with Rita Alvarez, who was a therapist at Jameson Hospital. She also did women's retreats at Janice's wellness center.

"Are you sure we should be seen leaving together?" April said in a low voice as they made their way to say goodbye to the Sullivan family.

"Are you ashamed to be seen with me?" Cole asked, wondering where she was going with that question.

"Of course not," she huffed. "I just know gossip travels fast in a small town and I didn't want to put you in an uncomfortable position."

"Don't worry about me. I can handle a few nosy neighbors."

She might have had a point. The speculative looks that Emily and her sisters gave them made him wonder how long he had until his mother asked him who that nice April girl was.

"I was thinking," she said as they walked toward their vehicles. "Since you've got to go to work this evening, why don't we head on over to my place. That way you don't have to kick me out when it's time for you to go."

"I wouldn't have kicked you out. You could have stayed as long as you like."

"That's sweet," she said. "But I think I want to be cuddled up in my own bed tonight."

"That works for me. Let me just stop by my apartment and grab an overnight bag."

She nodded, her hair falling in her face.

"Are you sure you're up for this? We don't have to do anything. I'm happy to watch Netflix and chill without the subtext if you just want to hang out."

"Nope." April reached down for his hand. "I'm all in."

His favorite phrase. He squeezed her hand. "Good."

They drove the short distance separately and parked by the school. "Want to come in?" he asked.

"Sure."

"Just don't look into the office as we go by. I don't want you to get distracted with paperwork."

"Not me," she said. "I'm Wild April now. Office April is out until Monday."

"Glad to hear it." He unlocked the door marked Private and led her up the stairs to his loft apartment.

"So, the whole top floor is yours?" she asked, leaning against the wall as he unlocked the door.

"See for yourself." Cole motioned her to go in front of him with a dramatic flourish. He couldn't help taking a quick look at her excellent backside as she went in.

The loft was set up with an open floor plan, except for the bathroom. Darting in there, he snagged a box of condoms and quickly brushed his teeth. As he stuffed a change of clothes into a duffel bag, Cole watched April walk around his place. She looked good here. She'd look even better in his bed. He was happy to see that her eyes drifted over to it a few times. Maybe he could convince her to take a long lunch up here with him next week.

"Why don't you live with your parents?" she asked.

He coughed out a laugh. "Because I'm thirty."

April giggled. "I mean it's such a big house and they obviously need to have you close. It could save you rent."

"Rent is included in my compensation for working here."

"That's a sweet deal," she said.

"Besides, I need a place to myself where I'm not on call twenty-four, seven."

"I can see that. I almost moved back in with my mother after I got laid off."

"Why didn't you?" He hoisted up the bag and gestured for the door.

She stared at the poker awards he had put up on a small shelf. He shifted uncomfortably. He should have had a World Series of Poker bracelet up there, too. He shook himself. Cole wasn't going there tonight. Not when he had a few hours to get lost in April's sweetness.

"I think we would have driven each other crazy," she said. "That and I think I'd cramp her style. I'm pretty sure she's having a fling with Mr. Jonas."

"Who's that?" He locked up behind them as they left the apartment and studio.

"He's the manager of the trailer park where she lives. I'm not sure how long it's been going on, or how long it's going to last. But for now, my mother seems happy. That's all that matters."

"But you think there might be romance in the air? That it's more than a fling?"

She gave a small laugh. "I'm not holding my breath. Mama falls in love like I change my shoes."

"What about you?" he asked.

"Me? I haven't really had time to even think about it. If it wasn't my sisters needing my attention, it was my job. Now, though?" She shrugged. "I'm open to whatever the universe is willing to provide."

Unfortunately, Cole wasn't able to provide much right now—which was how his life usually went.

APRIL KEPT CHECKING her rearview mirror, making sure that Cole was still behind her. She didn't want to risk losing him on the quick ride to the other side of town. She was nervous, even though she knew there was no reason to be. She trusted Cole and she'd been fantasizing about him all week. Her biggest challenge would be to keep this part of their relationship casual. Because she just wanted to jump up and down and dance naked in the moonlight.

Cole Lockwood was all hers.

At least for tonight.

That was all he was offering and damn it, she wasn't going to ruin it by overthinking. Wild April Grayson grabbed life by the reins and rode that wild pony around all the barrels without knocking them over.

"Damn right," she said aloud, just to add weight to her convictions.

As they pulled into her apartment complex, April hoped she hadn't left her bra hanging off the doorknob or something. She couldn't help trembling in giddy anticipation, and nearly dropped her keys while she got out of the car.

Cheddar was there to greet her when she opened the door to the apartment, but after taking one look at Cole, she darted under the couch.

"Don't mind her," April said as they walked inside. "She likes to pretend she's shy."

April's quick glance around the room assured her that everything was as tidy as she had left it and Cheddar hadn't decided to barf up a hairball. However, as she turned back to Cole, she noticed that he was looking at the planner she had left open on the coffee table. She resisted the urge to lunge for it. Instead, she just braced for his questions.

"You have a things-to-do list, with steps you need to take to become more like your sisters?" He cocked his head at her and a small smile flitted about his lips.

"It's like a bucket list and a countdown to my cruise, all rolled into one." She smoothed her hands down the sides of her sundress. This wasn't how she had been planning the evening to begin. "I was figuring I'd have a better time on my cruise if I got a few of those skills under my belt first."

"Pole dancing?" He quirked an eyebrow.

"I start lessons next week."

"Can I watch?"

The heat in his eyes mesmerized her. "Not until I get good."

"How is that going to help you enjoy yourself out in the middle of the Atlantic?"

"Cruises offer a lot of opportunities to go dancing, and I want to experience everything I can. I know there won't be a pole involved at the clubs onboard, but knowing that I've got the training will make me more confident to go to any of them."

Cole just frowned and continued to read down the list. "Find a fancy party to dress up for."

"They have formal nights on the cruise, and I want to make sure I can walk in, dressed to the nines, without ripping seams or breaking my ankle."

"You're very prepared for this."

"I try to be. Although sometimes it feels like I'm managing my own spontaneity."

"Go skinny-dipping?" His eyebrows rose. "I think they frown at that on cruise ships."

"Well," she said, wringing her hands. "I want to go into the pool and the hot tub and there's bound to be a bunch of strangers. I figure if I can skinny-dip in a creek around here, climbing into a hot tub wearing a one-piece bathing suit shouldn't be a problem."

"You don't have to go on this cruise alone."

April's shoulders slumped. "I pretty much have to. It's very expensive—I've been saving up for most of my life. But even if it wasn't, it's still a month long. I don't know anyone who has that much vacation time saved up who'd consider blowing it all in one shot."

Cole gave a noncommittal grunt.

"I'll be all right by the time the cruise rolls around. I've got a whole year to get ready."

"Have you ever thought about just taking a two-week cruise every year until you've seen all the sights you wanted to? That might be easier for a friend to manage."

The truth was there wasn't anyone she wanted to share a cabin with on a two-week cruise, never mind a full month. But she didn't want to tell him that, so she just shook her head. "No."

Another grunt.

"Can I get you a drink?" she asked, shyly.

"I better not. I'll fall asleep." Cole trailed a finger down the planner and April shivered as if he had done that down her spine instead. "I'd be happy to help you out with this list."

"Yeah," she said, hearing her voice sound low and husky.

"Go horseback riding with me."

Well, that wasn't at all what she was expecting—even though it had been on her list. "I would rather do other things with you." There, that had to be a big enough hint.

"We can do those, too," Cole said as he eased out of his shirt.

She forgot to breathe as his bare arms flexed when he went to the buckle of his jeans. Stepping closer, April tentatively touched his biceps. Then she curved her whole hand around the muscles in his arms.

"I love looking at you," she admitted.

He brought her over to the couch, where he took off his boots. "I like working in the same office as you. Your perfume gets me hard."

Cupping his face, she kissed him slowly, tasting his lips and letting her tongue play with his. He thumbed her nipple through her sundress. April pressed closer to him, her hand covering the hard bulge in his jeans, then rubbed him as the kiss got more intense. Cole slipped the strap of her sundress off and palmed her breast. The callouses on his hands against her sensitive skin made her insides quiver.

"I like how you touch me," she said, her lips feeling full and pouty.

"You're beautiful," he said hoarsely and dipped his head down to capture her nipple in his mouth.

Clutching his head to her breast, April closed her eyes as the tugging sensations shot straight to her clit.

"More," she moaned. Hiking up her dress, she straddled him.

Chuckling, he held her tight and went back to kissing her mouth. When he suddenly stood up, she shrieked and wrapped her legs around him.

"Bedroom?" he gasped between kisses.

She pointed frantically before going back to kissing him. Cole nudged open the bedroom door with his foot and walked her over to the bed. When he set her down, she whipped her sundress over her head. But before it could hit the floor, Cole's body pinned her to the bed. She used her feet to slide his jeans down his narrow hips.

"Yeah," he grunted, using her motion to tip her ankles over her head. "Hold them there."

She did while he chucked off his pants and underwear. He was gloriously naked in front of her and he laid his thick cock against the wet silk of her panties, then rocked against her, pulling her legs back to him.

"This is a lot more comfortable than last time," she joked.

"Good," he said. His voice was smoky with desire and his pretty blue eyes were sleepy and cloudy with lust. "I can't wait to slip inside you."

April squirmed, trying to edge her panties aside so he could. But instead of easing aside the barrier, he stretched himself over her and thrust as if they were making love. Clutching his ass, she rode him using the bump and glide against her clit to come—just like she'd done in the truck.

Sighing and moaning, she kissed him desperately, chasing the quick release. When he rolled to the side, that delicious friction was gone. But before she could complain, Cole moved her panties aside and plunged his fingers inside her. She gasped and pumped her hips up to take them deeper.

He fucked her with his fingers, and the slick sounds he made as he drove them in fast was as erotic as the little groans he let out at her eagerness. Easing off, he stroked her clit as she lay there shaking and panting.

Clamping her legs shut at the assault on her senses, she gripped his shoulders.

"Do you want me to stop?" he asked.

"I can't take it," she said. "So good."

Cole kissed down her body and spread her legs. "It is so good."

April shook apart as soon as his tongue lapped at her. He scooped up her hips and dove in between her legs like a man possessed. She could only lie back and stare at her ceiling as wave after wave of pleasure crashed into her. At one point, she arched into him, hips pumping against his face until she shuddered through an orgasm that she thought would shatter her into a thousand pieces.

Flipping her over, Cole nudged between her legs. "I'm putting on a condom now and then I'm going to fuck you until I come."

April was boneless and nodded against her pillow. He eased her up on her hands and knees and slid his thick cock through the sensitive folds he had just kissed as thoroughly as he had her mouth. Her fingers clawed at the sheets as Cole started slow, testing her reaction, seeing how deep he could go.

"More," she gasped.

He thrust deeper and faster. Hands on her hips, he pounded into her, the slap of their bodies the only sound in the room aside from their harsh breathing. April was still riding the thrill his tongue had caused when new sensations overcame her. His fingers dragged through her hair as he tugged her head back, while his other hand held her hips close to him.

"You're so tight," he muttered in her ear. "I swear I'm going to die."

"Don't stop," she pleaded.

"Not until I feel that sweet pussy come again."

His words made her clench her muscles against him and his harsh grunt almost pushed her over the edge again.

"So close," he gritted out.

She nodded, arching up to meet each thrust.

"Yes."

The sheets grazed her nipples each time he entered and retreated. She clamped down tight and rode it out as a scream left her throat with the force of the joy drenching her. She went limp as pleasure filled her. Cole's finishing strokes made him sound incoherent and as out of control as she felt. He collapsed on top of her, breathing heavily and cursing under his breath in shock and amazement.

"Yeah, me too," she chuckled.

After a moment, he eased out of her and went into the bathroom. She ducked under the covers and set her alarm clock to go off at seven thirty p.m.

"Come here," she said, peeling back the blankets when he came back.

Cole eased between them. "Hello, beautiful," he said, scooting in close.

"I set the alarm, so don't worry if you fall asleep."

"I'm not wasting a moment of this." He lay on his back and pulled her on top of him, then rubbed his big, calloused hands up and down her body while she trailed kisses over his neck and chest. Soon, though, his hands slowed, and his breathing grew deep and even.

Only then did April allow her eyes to flutter shut.

Chapter Twelve

C OLE HAD JUST finished unloading a truckful of hay into the cattle barn when his boss, Rick Braxton, poked his head in.

"Why don't you take a dinner break?" he said.

Stifling a yawn, Cole said, "I'm all right. What's up next?"

When he stepped out of the barn, April stood there with a large cooler in her hand.

"I think you and your girl are going to have a picnic. Why don't you drive up to the creek and enjoy the sunset?" Rick said.

"April?" Cole couldn't believe she was standing here in front of him. It had been hell to leave her, all cute and snuggled up in her bed, to get on a horse and ride all night long. The feel of her on his body had long since faded after a too quick sleep and working hard in the sun all day. And now looking at her in her tight jeans and T-shirt, he was dying to get the feel of her back.

"Mama cooked enough for an army," she said, swinging the cooler. "I hope you like beef stew."

"If he doesn't, I do," Rick called over his shoulder as he

walked back into the barn.

"Not a chance," Cole said to him. He walked over to April and gave her a kiss. "It's good to see you."

She kissed him back, lingering long enough that he considered another round in the truck with her instead of dinner.

"I hope you don't think I'm being pushy. I was worried you wouldn't have anything good to eat."

He didn't. On his way to work, he had stopped by the gas station and picked up a sandwich that had seen better days. He was relieved he wouldn't have to eat it. "You're a lifesaver. If you want, we can ride the horses out to the creek." The last thing his ass wanted was to be back in the saddle, but he needed to show her that she had nothing to fear from a well-trained horse.

April took a step back. "Nope. I'll drive."

He sighed. It had been worth a try. "Come on, let's take my truck."

A few minutes later, the truck was bouncing down the dusty path to the creek. Cole reached over and took her hand. "You do know how to ride a horse, right?"

She snatched her hand back. "Of course I can. I know how to take care of one, too. I just don't like to. I don't like them. My mother's pony Tulip, in fact, nearly killed me today."

"You were almost killed by a pony?" he said, trying to picture it.

"I see what you're thinking." April waggled her finger at him. "I'm not talking some Shetland pony. I'm talking a full-grown, mean-as-hell riding pony. Luckily, she loves apples more than she wants to take a bite out of me. When she charged, I tossed an apple in the other direction and she went after it instead. I was able run to the back door before she finished and came back after me."

"Why were you in the pen to begin with?"

April sighed. "My mother needed me to pick some beets and carrots from her garden and it's shorter to go through the pen than around it."

"Maybe Tulip was lonely."

"Maybe Tulip hates me," April said. "She doesn't try that trick with anyone else."

"You've trained her to expect food when she sees you."

"This is not my fault," she said hotly.

"I didn't mean it like that. I think it's less that she hates you and more that she wants the treat you've got on you."

"She tries to bite me if I don't give her anything."

"You guys should have taught her that was wrong a long time ago."

"We've tried everything. She's a cunning little monster and my mother spoils her rotten."

Cole grimaced. "It's hard to train a horse when there's no consistency. Have you ever stood your ground when she charged you?"

"Are you nuts? She's twelve hands high and weighs about five hundred pounds. Tulip used to give pony rides at rodeos. Mama fell hard for her owner." April tilted her head up and looked at the truck's ceiling. "I don't even remember his name. Jock? Jack? I don't know. They hooked up for a few seasons. He went to rodeos and state fairs with his portable fence and his two ponies. Tulip was one of them. Mama fell in love with her. So when she and Jock/Jack broke up, he gave Tulip to her."

"That was nice of him."

"Probably because by that time, Tulip would only listen to Mama. When the venues would allow it, we would take Tulip and a portable fence to give pony rides. Tulip let Mama and my sisters walk her with a child on her back, easy as you please. If I tried to walk her around the ring, she'd kick or bite. And she's only gotten worse in her old age."

"Why do you think she has it in for you?" Cole asked.

"It probably has to do with the pony cart I hooked her up to, years ago. My sisters and I were just kids, so our weight wasn't a problem. But Tulip hated the cart harness. I always started hitching her up, but Merry and June had to finish it because Tulip would act up. We should have read her reactions better, but we were just kids. And then she nearly killed the three of us when we tried to have her pull us in the cart."

Cole winced. "Where was your mother?"

"Working. June and Merry landed well. I broke my arm and the cart was trashed. Tulip was fine, though."

"Horses don't usually hold grudges."

"Tulip has a long memory."

Cole parked the truck and found an old horse blanket behind his seat that they could sit on. April helped him spread it out by the creek bed. It was just about sunset and he couldn't have planned a more romantic date if he tried.

It grated on his nerves that he'd have to be back at work in an hour, but these stolen moments were sweeter because they were so unexpected. He stifled a groan as he sank down on the ground. His arms and legs ached, but it was worth it to have April next to him.

"This is one heck of a surprise," he said. "I'm happy to see you."

"I should have brought a bottle of wine instead of lemonade," she fretted.

"Wine would have put me down for the count." He gestured with the lemonade bottle she handed him. "This hits the spot." Stretching out, he glanced over at April as she laid out some bowls and a basket of biscuits. He could get used to this.

"It's pretty here," she said.

Cole pushed a strand of hair that had fallen into her face back behind her ear. "You're pretty."

"I wasn't fishing for compliments," she said, her tone as tart as the lemonade.

"Noted." He snagged a biscuit. It was still warm. "I am grateful that you saved me from a gas station sandwich."

Wrinkling her nose up, she handed him a bowl of stew that he knew he was going to polish off like a starved wolf. "No one deserves that. I bet it had wilted lettuce."

"I didn't notice. I wouldn't have noticed. It's hard to care about what you're eating when you're driving a tractor."

"You work too hard," she said, placing a hand on his arm.

"Bills don't pay themselves." The end of the month was

coming and there were three past-due notices still hanging over his head.

"I was thinking… And at the risk of sounding like I'm giving unwanted financial advice…" She paused waiting for his response.

"Go ahead," Cole said, trying to cover up the gurgle his stomach made when the garlicky smell of beef hit him.

"Eat up first," she said, ladling herself a serving of stew.

Cole dug in and it tasted as good as it smelled.

"Can you consolidate all the bills and pay it off with a loan? That way you're just worried about one bill."

He thought about it while chewing. When he was done, he said, "There's not a lot of collateral left. My dad sold off most of the land and the house is mortgaged to the hilt."

"Can you sell the house?"

Cole almost dropped the soup bowl in shock. "What? Are you kidding me? That house was one of the first ones built in Last Stand."

"That's good," she said, rubbing her hands together. "You'll be able to leverage that for a higher selling cost. If you got an interested buyer, you could pay off the mortgage and the bills."

"No," he said firmly. "Just no."

"Really? Wouldn't your parents be happier in a ground-floor apartment closer to town?"

"It's not going to happen. Even if I could find a buyer in this market, my family's history is wrapped up in that house."

"It's just a house," April said.

"Not to my parents, it's not."

"Okay, I'm sorry. It was just a thought. I can see it's a sore spot for you."

"No," he groaned. "I'm sorry. I didn't mean to bite your head off. I'm tired and cranky. Just ignore me. Thank you for trying to help." He pulled her in for a kiss. She turned away at the last minute and he got her cheek. He supposed he deserved that for barking at her suggestion.

"The stew's fantastic," he said, trying for a truce.

"It's my mother's specialty. She makes enough to freeze, so we can enjoy it whenever we want a bit of comfort food." April fiddled with her napkin. "She's trying to get permission to bring some to June at the rehab center. Merry wound up telling her because Mama had been suspicious about why June had missed Emily's big announcement."

"She must have been upset."

April gestured to the food. "Hence all the cooking. But I think Mama was a little relieved. June was spiraling out of control. I think whatever happened scared the hell out of June. This could be the best thing for her. I'm hoping, anyway."

They finished up the stew in silence. The sun was going down and the pinks and oranges in the sky turned the creek into something out of a fantasy movie. Suddenly, Cole got an idea on how to brighten up the dreary turn of conversation. "Well, at least we're going to cross something off that bucket list you showed me the other day, the one with the steps you feel you need to take to be a real Wild Grayson." Then he kicked off his boots, and began stripping off his clothes.

"Cole," she shrieked.

He paused after kicking his pants off. "You wanted to build up your confidence. Skinny-dipping is the perfect way to start."

April just stared at him, her eyes riveted on his body. It made him hard when she licked her lips. He thought back to the other things he'd glimpsed on her bucket list, and wished he'd been able to read the whole thing through before April had caught him. Because suddenly, he wanted to know everything that was on that list more than he wanted to breathe. And he wanted to be the one to experience whatever she thought she needed with her.

"Is sex on a cruise ship on there?" he asked as jealousy reared up in the back of his head.

"Having sex outside is. But you know that already. Want to know what else is there?"

"Shit yeah, but I only have a half hour. We'll go over your list in detail later. Now, get out of those clothes and come join me." And before he lost his nerve, he climbed up on the big rock and jumped in.

It was chilly.

Pushing to the surface, he saw April was still there gaping at him.

"Don't make me come back there for you."

She leapt to her feet and looked around. "Are you sure there isn't anyone to see us?"

"No. And we'll hear them coming long before they get here."

April took her time taking off her shoes. "Are there snakes in there?"

"No. And no sharks either. Come on. We can do this more slowly later."

"Where have I heard that before?" she grumbled.

He treaded water as he watched her ease out of her clothes and fold them neatly in a pile.

"Today," he groaned, enjoying the sight of her sweet curves.

She gingerly made her way up the rock.

"You'll be fine."

"Don't let me drown."

"You're safe with me," he vowed.

She took a deep breath, which did mouthwatering things to her breasts. He could look at her toned legs and bitable ass all day.

"Is it cold?" she asked, shivering.

"No," he lied.

Squinching up her eyes, she took a running leap and landed next to him with a tremendous splash. Reaching for her, he grabbed her hand and pulled her up.

"Dirty, rotten liar. I'm freezing my tits off," she shouted.

"I hope not." He cupped his hands over them.

April wrapped her legs around his waist. "I'm going to get you for this."

But his eyes crossed when her sweet bottom brushed up against his cock. Just a few adjustments and he'd be inside her. Cole shifted her away before the temptation got to him. "It's refreshing."

"It would have been a lot more refreshing when the sun was up," she grumbled, unaware of the effect she was having on him.

"The sun's still up. At least for a few more minutes. Let's enjoy it while it lasts." He kicked his legs and floated on his back with her still wrapped around him. She refused to let go. Normally, he'd love that, but for now, he was trying to get them back to where he could touch the bottom.

"So, what did you think?" he asked when he had solid footing.

"It is a bit colder than I imagined," she said, squirming to keep most of her body under water. "But I'm getting used to it."

And he was getting used to the smooth feel of her body against his. If he wasn't careful, he'd carry her out of the creek and make love to her on the scratchy old horse blanket and then be late back from supper break.

"Let's play around." He unwrapped her from around him, reluctantly, then hoisted her up out of the water and tossed her back in a few feet away.

"No fair." She came up spluttering and splashing.

He let her chase him around for a bit before letting her catch up and dunk him. He held up his hands in surrender. "I give up. I give up."

"You're lucky I'm merciful," she said.

"You're lucky I've got to get back to work." He lifted her back into his arms in a honeymoon carry and hauled them both out of the water. "We've got just enough time to dry off."

After setting her down on the blanket, he gathered up his clothes and swapped them with a clean set he had in his duffel bag.

"I don't suppose you have a towel in there," she called out.

"Sorry, but I could start carrying a few, if we're going to make this a thing."

"Yes. Do that." April flexed her toes and stared up at the darkening sky with her arms folded over her head.

"I'm sorry I'm always running out just when things are getting good."

"Come here. Dry off with me for a few more minutes."

Cole looked at his watch. He had the time. He eased next to her. "I want to lick those droplets off you," he said, propping himself up on his elbow.

"I'm not stopping you." She wiggled closer.

"There's never enough time," he said sadly and traced his finger over her quivering belly.

"There's enough time for this." April pushed him flat on his back and gripped his cock in her hands.

"Sweetheart," he protested weakly.

"You said you wanted to help me with my list." She pouted, stroking him up and down.

"I don't have condoms."

"We won't need them for this," she whispered and licked a slow circle around the tip.

Cole forgot how to form words. Then she slid him deep into the back of her throat before slowly easing back to the tip. He rang his fingers through her hair. "Amazing," he managed to whisper. Bending over him, she sucked him in and out of her mouth in a dizzying rhythm. Before his world narrowed down to that sweet sensation, Cole reached two fingers between her legs and tickled his way inside her where she was hot and slick. While she bobbed up and down on him, he played with her.

April squirmed and moaned around him, which was the hottest thing ever. He needed her to be as into this as he was because he was about to explode.

"Honey," he grunted as her body jerked in little spasms. She took him deeper, sucked him harder. "Coming," he warned and tried to move away, but her firm palm on his chest stopped him. He went off like a rocket and she hummed her approval. He knew his fingers were clumsy, but he felt she was satisfied by the way she rocked on them.

As she lifted her head up, April's face was flushed. "That'll do for now."

He removed his fingers and brought them up to his lips to taste her. "For now."

Chapter Thirteen

WILD APRIL GRAYSON was having a great Monday, even though she kept coming up with different sums in one column and her body ached a bit from playing around with Cole.

When she went to refill her coffee, Kelly was leaning up against the sink in the kitchenette. She had tears in her eyes and was rubbing her belly.

"Why didn't you tell me you were here? Are you all right?" April said, moving forward to give her a gentle hug.

"I wanted to get myself under control first."

"Why don't you sit down for a moment?" April said. "I can make you some tea."

"That would be nice." Kelly sounded so miserable that April's heart went out to her.

"I've missed you."

"Yeah, I haven't felt well enough to get out of bed."

"Why are you crying?" April asked, dropping a ginger tea bag into a mug.

"It's nothing really. Pregnancy hormones." Kelly took a bunch of tissues out of her pocket and dabbed at her nose.

After filling up the teakettle, April put it on the burner.

"That should be ready in a few minutes. I'm going to have a cup of chai."

"I love the smell of that." Kelly gave a watery grin. "How are things going? Has Trent's paperwork driven you crazy yet?"

"I've seen worse. I'm making headway. He'll be all caught up for tax season and I can make sure that he's prepared for next year as well."

"That's one less thing to worry about. Thank you."

"It's my job. How's your photography studio coming along?"

"Great. I got asked to do the Last Stand High School senior portraits. That's a big coup around here." She smiled briefly. "It's been a tough few years."

"Are things going better for the ranch?" April asked.

"Last year was so crazy, most of our plans were stalled. But Janice's retreat center has been booked solid for the last few months and Donovan is doing great, too. Emily is still keeping my dad in line while getting the wind turbines installed as soon as she can. It's busy and I'm happy to be working with my family. But some days..." She blew out a sigh. "It's too much."

April nodded. "Us middle sisters have to stick together."

"Exactly," Kelly said, nodding.

Once the water in the kettle was boiling, April poured it into the two waiting mugs. She put them on the small table with sugar and milk. Kelly used one teaspoon of sugar and a splash of milk. April put in a glug of milk and a tablespoon of sugar.

"I've got a sweet tooth." She shrugged.

"Me too. But I'm trying not to eat everything in sight. I want to, though. Anyway, thanks for the tea. I ducked in here because I didn't want to hear Donovan argue with Janice anymore."

"What are they arguing about?"

"Donovan's dad is kind of a shady character. He's renting Janice's retreat this month for a group of ex-cons who have been just released from long prison terms."

"Here?" April said, splashing her chai.

"Sorry," Kelly said. "I shouldn't have just dropped that on you. The ex-cons have been vetted. They're all white-collar criminals and have never hurt anyone physically. And they're all out on parole. Their parole officer will be there as well to keep an eye on them, and a couple of off-duty Last Stand policemen were hired to be security."

"So why are Donovan and Janice fighting?"

"Donovan and his dad are estranged. He thinks Janice should keep his dad from coming over to the hunting club to see him." Kelly took a sip of her tea. "Janice thinks Donovan needs to nut up—her words—and tell his father to piss off or hear him out. Donovan isn't doing either and it's making everyone a little crazy."

"That's complicated."

"The problem is that I can see both their sides," Kelly said. "And I hate getting caught in the middle."

"Me too." April thought about the countless times June and Merry had had spats and had insisted she take sides when all she'd wanted was to be left alone.

"Thanks for listening," Kelly said, rubbing her belly. "I'm going to go hide in Trent's office for a while. He dragged in an old recliner so I can sit with my feet up and look out the window. If you hear snoring, I apologize."

"Don't," April said. "Growing a baby is hard work."

"Yeah, but it's worth it. Still, I go from being scared to death that something is wrong to assuring myself that everything I'm feeling is perfectly normal."

"That's quite an emotional roller coaster," April said. She wasn't sure she'd be able to handle it. Hell, she was having a hard enough time just trying to loosen up.

"I had such grand ideas for this pregnancy," Kelly said. "I wanted to paint the nursery and listen to classical music. Now, I can barely keep my eyes open."

"Listen to your body," April said.

"I thought I'd be over this three months ago." Kelly gulped at her tea. "My body is being a jerk."

April pulled out a fresh box of shortbread cookies and handed her a sleeve.

"Thank you," Kelly said, snatching one up. She moaned in pleasure. "These cookies just melt in your mouth," she said, her mouth full. "I love the crystalized sugar too."

"How's Alissa handling things?"

"She's not happy that I'm not at her beck and call. I keep telling her how great it will be when the baby gets here. It's a good thing her aunts and her grandmother are around."

"It's a lot of change for one little girl to manage," April said, shaking her head.

"Change can be good."

Can it? April had to think about that. To her, change had always been a lot of trouble.

"I want Alissa to have sisters. I wouldn't have made it without mine."

"Sisters?" April said, shocked. "You're going to go through this another time, after this baby is born?"

"Three times is the charm."

"If you say so," April said. Then she smiled. "But you're right—sisters are pretty great."

"Even though they have their moments," Kelly grumbled.

"Truth." She tapped mugs with Kelly in solidarity.

"Have you heard anything from June?"

Shaking her head, April risked her life to steal a shortbread cookie from the pregnant lady. "She doesn't have her phone, which is probably killing her. Merry has taken on her promotions so her sponsors don't dump her...which means she's working too hard. And my mother is worried sick."

"I guess it's a good thing that you're close by."

April nodded. "I'm glad I'm back in Last Stand. As long as I can keep getting clients, I should be able to make ends meet and be back on schedule once tax season is over."

"Back on schedule?" Kelly asked, amusement lighting up her face.

"I've got to start saving to pay off my cruise and then..." April stopped mid-sentence.

"Well, don't keep me in suspense," Kelly drawled.

"I just realized I'm not really sure what I'm going to do after the cruise. I hadn't thought that far ahead yet."

Kelly clapped her hands together. "Finally. Good for you. Now, you're getting it."

Smiling self-consciously, April fiddled with the cookie box. What was next for her? Cole flitted around in her mind. She'd like to see if what they had could turn into something more meaningful.

"Oh." Kelly rubbed her forehead. "Pregnancy brain. The other reason why I'm here is to tell you that June's horse is in the stable by the main house. Merry made all the arrangements for a self-care board and said you'd be taking care of Athena."

"Athena's here already?" April almost choked on her chai. She wasn't ready for that. She figured she'd have another week or so to psych herself up for it.

"She got dropped off this morning with clean bedding and a month's worth of feed. So all you have to worry about is mucking out the stall and turning her out in the pasture."

Oh no. There was a lot more to worry about than that. Luckily, Kelly didn't notice how horrified April was.

"She's already been fed and watered, so you don't have to check on her until after work."

"Thanks," April said with a sigh.

Nodding, Kelly lumbered to her feet and took her tea into her husband's office. April was finishing up her tea and wondering how she was going to handle Athena all by herself when Cole popped his head in. He was smiling so wide, she wondered if he had won the lottery or something.

"Guess what?" he said.

"I can't imagine."

"We're crossing off another thing on your list Saturday night."

"Which list?" she asked, feeling the welcome heat of desire coil through her despite her impending sense of doom about having to deal with her sister's horse.

Cole's eyes grew dazed. "Both of them. But the one I was thinking of is the fancy dress part."

"You remembered," she said, touched that he thought it was important because she did.

"We're going to the Bluebonnet Country Club in San Antonio. It's very formal and really hoity-toity. You're going to have to practice walking around with your nose in the air."

"Ha," she said. "That's so not Wild April."

"Good."

"What's the occasion?"

"I've been invited to enter a high-stakes poker game and you are to be my arm candy."

"Excellent," she said, but then frowned. "High-stakes? I'm taking it this isn't nickel poker."

"No." Cole cleared his throat. "It's a Vegas level buy-in without the hassle of going to Vegas."

That sounded expensive. "I don't mean to be nosy, but I was under the impression that money was tight for you. Hence the day and night jobs."

"Poker is actually my third job."

"Poker is a fun game. It's not a valid way to make money," April said, gripping her cup. Gambling was fun. She liked to spend an hour or two at the slot machines and the tables, but after she lost, she usually wound up feeling sick to her stomach and thinking about what she should have spent the money on instead.

"Actually, for me it is. I made a decent living at it a few years ago."

"It's not sustainable," she said, trying for reason. He couldn't possibly be thinking of gambling with the money he'd worked so hard for, the money that he'd slated to pay his parents' medical bills. "And right now, it's not a good risk."

"You don't understand. It's a great risk because I'm really good at the game. Look, I can't get into the details right now. But please say you'll go with me?"

"Of course, I'll go." Maybe, she could reason with him so he didn't do something he regretted.

"Excellent. You'll be my lucky charm. And afterward, it'll be just you, me, and that sexy list."

"That sounds really great," she said.

"You don't sound convincing. You don't have to go with me if you don't want to."

She looked up at the resignation in his voice. "No, I do." Someone had to keep him from throwing all that money away. It was difficult to imagine herself getting involved with a gambler. She'd just have to keep telling herself that she wasn't her mother and Cole wasn't a douchebag.

"So why do you look like you just found a fly in your tea?"

April checked in her cup, just in case. She didn't want to get into a debate about gambling, so she chose the other topic that was bothering her right now. "I just found out June's horse is being boarded here. She arrived this morning. I'm surprised I didn't smell the sulfur and brimstone."

"Why didn't they board her at your mom's place with the pony from hell?"

April shook her head. "There's not enough room. Athena is better off here, but the catch is that I've got to take care of her."

"Is she a biter too?"

"No, June wouldn't stand for that. She's Ares's sister. Ares is the horse that nearly knocked my head off. She's not as violent, but she's a prima donna all the same, an escape artist who likes to be out in the pasture instead of in her stall."

Cole shrugged. "Let her stay out all day, then. She's not getting out of our pasture. Nate and Emily make sure that the fencing is top-notch. There's plenty of shade, water, and there probably will be a couple of the ranch hands' spare horses to keep her company.

"Yeah?" April said. That didn't sound so bad. She didn't mind mucking out the stall as long as that mare was far, far away.

"I'll even help you take a look at her hooves and check her out."

"Ugh, I hadn't even considered that. That would be a huge help. You're so busy, though. I don't want to take up any more of your time."

"It's ten minutes, tops. And maybe, I can convince you to take Athena for a ride."

April shook her head so violently, she almost gave herself whiplash. "No, she's hot as soon as you get astride her. Athena will likely take off like a shot and nicker when I fall off, or stop short, sending me flying over her head."

"That sounds like the voice of experience."

April considered wiping off his amused expression with a kiss, but that was probably unprofessional in the workplace. So, she stuck out her tongue at him instead.

"Promises, promises." Cole winked at her and then went back outside as his third class of the day was just arriving.

Unfortunately, by the time she pulled herself from Trent's books, it was getting dark and she figured Cole must have left for his night job. She drove down the long dirt road to the stable and saw Emily talking with her sister Janice.

"I'm sorry. I'm late, aren't I?"

"That's okay. Cole stopped by on his way out and took care of Athena," Janice said. "What a beauty."

"Cole or Athena?" April joked.

"Athena, but Cole's got some fine lines too."

"Janice!" Emily gasped mockingly. "I'm telling Nate."

"I'm a married woman, not a dead one." Janice smiled. "Besides Cole is Nate's number-one guy now because of the poker games he's bringing to Donovan's club. He's getting sick of playing with us and the ranch hands."

"The high-stakes game?" April asked. "I thought that was at a country club in San Antonio."

"There's going to be a high-stakes game one weekend every month, from what Donovan was telling me," Emily said. "But there could be other games going on with the crowd they were talking about bringing in. It sounded like a bunch of Texas millionaires with money to burn."

"Well, that leaves Nate out," Janice said. "The most he's ever brought to a poker game is a hundred dollars."

April nodded. "That seems reasonable." Of course, there were times when she'd been growing up that a hundred dollars was scarce. They would have had to use it on gas for the truck or put it toward a vet bill. That was why she couldn't figure out why Cole could gamble, using the money he needed. Maybe it was because he'd never really had to do without before? April was sure that the Lockwoods had never had to resort to eating ramen and bologna sandwiches in that big old house with all those empty rooms.

"Do you want to see Athena?" Janice said, walking into the stable.

Unable to think of a good excuse not to, April followed her.

"These two are my babies, Synergy and Black Dahlia," Janice said, giving each of them a fond pat.

Forcing a smile, April edged as far away from them as she could.

"This is Emily's horse Sunflower and Kelly's horse Pippi," Janice added. She continued walking toward the last stall. And there, at the end, was Athena.

April was surprised at the flood of emotion she felt seeing the bad-tempered mare. With a wash of nostalgia, she had to blink back tears. Athena wasn't June. But since she couldn't hug June right now, taking care of her horse might be the next best thing.

"Hello, asshole," she said to the animal.

Janice blinked in surprise.

"It's a pet name I have for her. She hasn't said anything, but I have a feeling she calls me the same thing."

Janice coughed a laugh and stroked the white star on Athena's brown forehead. "She's a hot horse. June gave us permission to ride her for exercise and Emily and I have been fighting over who gets to do it."

"Be my guest. Better you than me. Did Cole have a hard time getting her back into the stall?" April asked, already knowing the answer.

"Eventually. Once the other horses came back, she decided she'd allow Cole to bring her in."

"Oh no, I hope he wasn't late for work."

"I don't think so."

April sighed. "Well, I shouldn't keep you. I've got a dance lesson tonight anyway."

"What are you studying? Modern, jazz, ballet?" Janice shut off all the lights and locked up the stable behind them.

"Pole."

Janice stumbled. "What? But you're an accountant."

"Yes. And I'm also a Grayson," April said, proudly.

Chapter Fourteen

TODAY WAS THE day. Cole slept as well as he could with the old excitement pulsing through his veins. Thank goodness online poker games didn't fuel the adrenaline like in-person games. Still, he knew he had to keep busy and burn off some energy, otherwise he'd be strung out when it was time to sit at the table.

He headed over to the stable to take care of Athena. She was a beautiful animal, and he'd love a chance to bring her to the school to show the kids a great barrel racing horse. Cole wasn't sure if April would let him, but he wanted Athena to get used to him, just in case.

He was surprised to see that April was already there, wearing thigh-high mucking boots and barn clothes. "Good morning, sunshine."

Kissing her was an unexpected pleasure that he didn't think he'd get a chance to do until later. Her soft brown hair was pulled back in a ponytail and it made him want to wrap his hand around it and hold her to him. He enjoyed her soft mouth and the taste of her.

He would have liked to spend the day with her, but he had to work at his parents' neighbor's farm, filling in for a ranch hand today. A pang of wistfulness soured his mood, and he broke off the kiss. The land used to be part of the Lockwood estate, so Cole knew it well. Still, it would allow him to think about April when he wasn't planning his poker strategy. One of these days, he'd be out of debt and all he'd have to think about would be running wild with a wild Grayson sister.

"I wasn't expecting to see you here," he said.

"I told Merry I'd look after the asshole and I will." She grabbed a pitchfork.

He was proud of April. She was determined to take care of her sister's horse, despite her fear. "You need any help?"

"I told you, I've done this before," she said, leaning on the pitchfork. She didn't look like she was in a hurry to get in the stable.

"Why are you still out here then?"

"I'm trying to get up the courage to walk past the horses and lead Athena out."

"Do you want me to do it?"

She shook her head. "No, getting her out isn't the problem. Getting her back in will be."

"It's going to be a nice day. Let her stay out in the pasture if she wants. Janice will be down shortly to let the other horses out."

"Maybe they will improve Athena's attitude," April muttered.

"I know you're used to ornery horses," Cole said. "But the Sullivan horses are well trained. Pippi and Sunflower are the gentlest beasts I've ever seen. Emily and Kelly let me borrow them for the kids who are intimidated by the horses we have at the school."

"They are pretty," she had admitted grudgingly. "Their names fit too. Sunflower is bright yellow like the flower she was named after, and Pippi is reddish brown with dark freckles on her torso. I'm babbling, aren't I?"

"You can stay out here and babble, if you want."

"No, I don't have all day." Straightening her shoulders, April turned and walked into the stable.

Cole remained back as she led Athena out. April was gripping the harness so tightly, her knuckles were white. Athena was in high spirits, but was behaving herself. Cole opened the pasture gate and closed it behind them, just in case the mare got it in her head to be difficult. But Athena was content to let April check her over. She stomped once and snorted, but stopped when April cussed her out.

"She's on her best behavior," Cole noted, coming in to hold the halter while April checked her hooves. He didn't like that April was stone-faced and shaking.

"That's because she's not used to these surroundings. She's high-strung, but then again, so is June. I guess that's why they work so well together."

"What's Merry's horse like?"

"Raphael—my sister was on an angel kick when she named him—is a gelding. He only works when Merry's riding him. But at least he's not looking for a chance to misbehave. Not like this girl."

She took the lead off and stepped back. Athena took off as if April had swatted her butt.

"Fast." Cole nodded in approval.

April grunted and headed back to the stable.

"Did you ever have a horse?" he asked, grabbing another pitchfork to help.

"Not for long."

"So, did you ride Athena or Raphael?"

She shook her head. "Nope. We got them both at the same time we got Ares. He was the only horse for me. My first…and my last."

Cole winced.

"I'm a lousy rider anyway. I've got a bad seat and I don't have any patience."

"Careful. It sounds like you're getting soft on them."

"Never. Horses are just so big, and I'm a bundle of nerves whenever I'm too close to them."

"But do you think you could get used to them?"

"I don't know," she said.

"Maybe if you had a horse of your own, it would be different. Maybe a sweet gentle one like Pippi or Sunflower could change your mind."

"I don't see the need to have a horse in my life right now. I'm not paying to board one. And I'm certainly not stabling one with Tulip, even if there was room." April shuddered.

"I have to meet this Tulip."

"Save a Sunday and you can come over for lunch."

"I'd like that." He wondered if she realized they were getting a little more serious. After all, meeting the parents was a big step.

"Mama would be thrilled. She'll probably flirt outrageously. Ignore her. It's just her way."

"Is your dad around?"

April shrugged. "Not since I was a kid. I don't even think I'd recognize him if I saw him again. He was just one of many who my mom fell in love with. I think he's a ranch hand in Dallas now, but I don't know for sure."

"I'm sorry. That must have been rough, growing up without a father around."

"There were plenty of other fathers. June's father stuck around for a couple of years. Merry's lasted the longest and even came back a few times." April closed her eyes and thought. "There were a few more cowboys before Jack/Jock and a few after. They didn't stay either. In the end, they weren't important enough for me to remember their names. At least they were all good guys for the most part. I mean, you hear horror stories about a mother's boyfriends abusing the kids. That never happened. It was more indifference or grudging acceptance that we felt. Mama was the one who always kept us in line, anyway. There was no need for anyone else."

Cole didn't know what to say, but he admitted he understood the wild Grayson sisters a little better now. "You had to grow up fast, though."

"We all have to grow up sometime." She dusted off her hands when they finished cleaning Athena's stall. "I've got no complaints."

Cole could have offered a few—mainly about the ways she'd had to be the responsible one while her mother and sisters lived a carefree life full of fun. He supposed that was why she was trying to make up for lost time.

"Cole, I've been thinking about this high-stakes poker game." She pulled off her gloves and put the pitchfork back. "Are you sure you want to risk that much money when you have bills to pay?"

"Unfortunately, the ten thousand dollars stake money I've got won't put much of a dent in them."

"Ten thousand," April choked out.

Holding a hand up to stop her protests, he said, "But if I can triple that amount in this game, it will pay for last year's chemo bill for my father. Hell, it could even take care of Gwen's, our home health aide's, salary for the rest of the year."

"Don't you have insurance?" April gasped.

"That's after insurance," Cole said kindly. "I also have my mother's gall bladder surgery bills that we're trying to stay ahead of by paying them off slowly."

"I was going to try and convince you to invest it, but the most I could see you getting is a five percent return in a year." April looked so forlorn Cole couldn't help but offer solace. He caressed her cheek.

"I'm going to get a three hundred percent return on my investment tonight."

"Or you could lose it all." She threw herself into his arms so hard he had to take a few steps back.

Rubbing her back, Cole put his chin on the top of her head. They fit right together. "I'm good at this. I like doing it and I'm smart about betting. I know you've never seen me in action, so I'm going to have to ask you to trust me. I know how this works. I need you to be my good luck charm, though. That means no more talk about me losing. At least, not until after the game, okay?"

"Okay." She sniffed and then let go. Clasping his arms, she forced a smile. "I believe in you."

"That's all I need to hear."

WHEN APRIL TOLD her mother she was going to San Antonio that night, Mama made a sound of pure joy. And then she ordered April to come home for a makeover. And that was how she found herself sitting on a chair in the center of the family room with her own team of beauticians. Her mother had called in everyone from Clippety-Do-Da who wasn't working.

April had had a manicure and a pedicure, which had been really nice. The eyebrow and chin plucking hadn't been so good, though, and she'd absolutely drawn the line at the Brazilian wax. Her mother had insisted she be allowed to lighten April's highlights and April had to admit, they came out spectacular.

While her mother braided her hair in an intricate pattern that made her look like a storybook princess, April's makeup was being done by her mother's best friend Samantha, who used to do Merry and June's makeup when they were rodeo queens.

Was this her rodeo queen moment?

"Stop blinking or the mascara will smear all over your

cheeks." Samantha scowled at her.

"I wish I could go with you," her mother sighed. "The Bluebonnet Country Club."

Samantha snorted. "Penny, you'd get thrown out as soon as you started stuffing crab legs into your purse. Just like you did at the Crab King buffet."

"That was thirty years ago. Would you let it go already?"

Dusting a finishing powder over April's face, Samantha said, "Cole Lockwood's a good catch. Nice family. Nice money. And he's not too hard to look at."

"I haven't caught him. We're dating." Sort of. They were working up to dating. But she didn't want her mom's friends gossiping about her sleeping around with a boy from the other side—the better side—of the tracks. Not like that sort of stuff mattered anymore. Or did it? She wondered if Cole's family would be uncomfortable if he brought home one of the wild Grayson sisters.

"What do you know about the Lockwoods, Samantha?" she asked.

Samantha gave a half shrug as she critically looked over her handiwork. "I don't run in their circles, but I hear they're okay."

"Do you think they'd like me?" April asked.

"What kind of nonsense is that?" her mother said. "They'll love you. And if they don't, what do you care? You're marrying their son, not them."

"Mama!" April almost bolted out of the chair. "This is like our fourth date. Don't jinx it."

"I just hope he goes on that cruise with you next year."

Folding her arms in front of her, April settled back into the chair. "That's not going to happen."

"I'm worried about you being so far away, all by yourself."

"I'll be fine, Mama. I'm the sensible one anyway."

"Well, you used to be." Her mother handed her a mirror.

April barely recognized herself. She didn't look like June. She didn't look like Merry. She looked like Wild April Grayson about to go on an adventure.

"Don't you dare cry. If you ruin your makeup, I'm not going to fix it," Samantha scolded.

Chapter Fifteen

C OLE WAS GLAD he'd decided to rent a Mercedes for the evening. The actual players might not see him toss the keys to the valet, but it helped in making him feel like he belonged here. And it didn't hurt his confidence that April was a knockout at his side. The fancy dress she wore plunged low in the front and even lower in the back. Glistening white stones outlined her cleavage and he'd knew he'd have to make sure she was standing behind him, so he didn't get distracted during the game.

"I can't wait to get you out of that dress," he said in her ear.

She shivered in reaction.

He took the time to nuzzle her bare neck. Her hair was piled up on top of her head in an intricate style. "You look beautiful."

"Thanks. When Mama found out where you were taking me tonight, she called in all her friends from the beauty shop and they gave me the Cinderella treatment."

"Welcome to the ball, Cindy." He spread his hand out, indicating the marbled floor and the giant fountain in the reception center.

After he tucked her arm into his, they leisurely followed the signs leading them to the gaming tables.

"Invitation, sir?" The doorman to the room held out a white-gloved hand.

Reaching into the inside pocket of his tuxedo jacket, Cole handed the man the green and black envelope that allowed him and a guest into the pit area.

"Good luck, sir," he said with an incline of his head.

As they stepped inside and the door closed behind them, Cole immediately felt at ease. It could have been Vegas. There were smokers at the table, but the air filtration system was so state of the art, he couldn't catch even a hint of cigarette or cigar smell. The cashier was off to the left and he headed that way to get his chips.

April clung to him, but didn't say anything when he confirmed the tray was full of ten thousand dollars' worth of chips.

"I'll have your chips delivered to table three," the cashier said. "We're starting in a half hour. Please enjoy the complimentary bar and buffet."

Yeah, just like Vegas. Still, it was hard to watch the money walk away. But that wasn't the right way to think. That money was a tool—not a month's worth of payment plans. He was going to go big or go home.

"This place is off the charts," April said.

"Ritzy enough to cross off the list?"

"Definitely."

"Is caviar on your bucket list too?" Cole asked, looking down at the buffet table.

"No, but maybe it should be."

He put a little on a cracker and fed it to her. "What do you think?"

She thought about it as she chewed. "Too fishy. And not dangerous enough to make my bucket list."

Chuckling, he handed her a plate. "What's dangerous? Are we talking hot sauce or exotic?"

"I don't know. My sisters dared me to try Rocky Mountain oysters. I didn't have the guts. Something like that."

He gave her a side eye. "You do know they're not oysters, right?"

"I didn't at the time, until a vaquero my mother was dating called them *huevos de toro*. Thank you, high school Spanish class. Have you ever tried them?"

"They're chewy. Nothing I'd order as a favorite, but at least I can say I tried them. I don't see anything exotic on the buffet, but I'm pretty sure you can put in an order and they'll get it for you."

"You think?"

He liked that she thought that was being daring and naughty. "There's one way to find out. What's your pleasure?"

"I'm not sure." She cocked her head in thought.

"In Vegas, you can order Decadence D'Or cupcake from The Palazzo. It's drizzled with expensive cognac and topped with gold vanilla caviar."

"In a cupcake?" April put her hand over her face.

"With edible gold flakes sprinkled on top."

"Of course," she said. "But I like my cupcakes sans fish."

"Crispy tarantulas."

April recoiled. "Are you high? Hard no."

"White ant soup."

Swatting him with the plate, she grimaced. "Are you trying to make me throw up? Don't tell me you've tried either of those."

"No, not me. Emily mentioned that when she was in the Peace Corps, the locals tried to get her to eat those dishes, but she managed to get out of it because she was a vegetarian."

"I'd claim to be a vegetarian, too."

Cole racked his brains for another. "You could ask for some Kobe beef over there. It comes from Wagyu cows that get sake baths and daily massages."

"I would, but I wouldn't want to offend these Texas cattlemen."

He kissed her hand. "Thoughtful as well as beautiful."

After a quick tour around the table, Cole decided on a steak and lobster tail meal with a huge baked potato. He wanted something to last him for most of the night. If all went well, he'd have a post-midnight sandwich that would tide him over until a celebratory breakfast.

April went for a lighter fare of cocktail shrimp and clams casino, with a few stuffed mushrooms that he was probably going to go back and try if there was time.

They sat down on the third floor that overlooked the pit area. A few private games were going on and if he was smart, he'd be watching the players to see if he could identify their tells. He might not even be playing them, though, and he wanted to enjoy this time with April.

"Have you played in places like this before?" she asked, digging into her dinner with gusto.

Cole liked that about her. She did everything with joy. "No, but my parents had a membership here for a while. They have a golf course and a pool."

"Of course, they do," she said, looking down at her plate. "Did you have fun here?"

"For a little while. There's only so much swimming and tennis that you can do in between school and chores."

"Did you ever feel uncomfortable or out of place?" she asked.

"No, everyone seemed to know everyone."

"Do you know anyone here?" April asked.

Scanning the room, Cole didn't see anyone who looked familiar. He caught the eye of one man who seemed to know him, though. The man raised his glass, saluting Cole. Cole smiled and nodded.

"Not really, but someone knows me."

"He looks familiar," April said. "I've seen him around Last Stand, but I don't know who he is. Maybe he'll come over and introduce himself." She gave him a smile and went back to her food, but he noticed she was playing with her stuffed mushroom instead of eating it.

Before he could ask her what was wrong, the waitress came over to take their drink order. April ordered a gin and tonic, but Cole stuck to water. Later, he'd switch to coffee.

"How is the pole dancing going? I want a personal demonstration," he said.

"Unless Trent installs a pole in the school, I don't think that's going to happen."

"We can improvise. Maybe with a fence post."

"You could come to my dance school and observe."

"I'd feel like a creeper," he said.

"If I get good at it, maybe I'll install one in my apartment. Only for exercise purposes, of course." She grinned at him.

He was happy to see that her appetite had come back and he dug into his own dinner. "Works for me." He reached across the table and held her hand. "I'm glad we connected at Buddy's. I like seeing you every day at work. I'm going to miss that when you finish with Trent's paperwork."

"That's still a month or so away. I don't want to think too closely about that. I need to be more diligent about building a client list."

"One of the things my parents still have to worry about is their taxes. I know I mentioned this before, but maybe we should hire you."

"I'd be happy to take a look, but they might not need me. I do a free consultation with all my potential clients. It's like a job interview. If I could find them a few deductions for medical expenses, I'd be glad to help."

"Tell you what. I'll help you get over your fear of horses in return for the free consultation."

April speared a mushroom into her mouth, and gave him a fishy look.

"I know you don't like horses, but it was on your first list as something you wanted to manage. And I know it can't be easy, being intimidated by them either. I'm not trying to make you into a barrel racer, but I wouldn't mind a riding partner on a sultry summer night."

"I really don't like horses."

"I get that, but maybe you haven't been exposed to the right ones. Don't let Tulip or your sisters' horses control you anymore. A wild Grayson sister, after all, is known for being on horseback."

April narrowed her eyes at him. "I'm a bad rider," she hedged, but he thought she was warming to the idea.

"I can teach you to be a better one. Ask all my sixth graders. It's what I do for a living."

"When you're not playing poker in glamorous locations like a modern-day James Bond."

"I knew I should have found an Aston Martin to rent." Cole gently banged on the table.

"Where do you keep your Walther PPK?"

"Put your hand in my pocket and I'll show you."

When April looked around, he thought she would actually do it. But she settled back with her gin and tonic instead. "So, tell me what I'm going to be watching tonight."

"Have you ever seen poker on television?"

"Nope," she said, shaking her head.

"Okay, real quick. We're playing a game called Texas hold 'em. Everyone gets two cards dealt face down. Those are called your pocket cards. And then there's five community cards that everyone shares to make their best hand."

"So if you have two threes in your pocket cards and a three shows up in the community cards, you'd have three of a kind."

"Trip threes," he said. "But the way to win is not necessarily having the best hand. It's how you read people and how they bet."

"Sounds a little new-age mystical woo-woo," she said, wiggling her fingers.

"It's actually science and math."

"Oh, how boring. I like my description better."

A soft chime sounded. "Players, please take your seats," the announcer said, followed by another chime.

This was it. Go big or go home.

Cole pushed his chair back and caught April's lips in a quick kiss. "For luck."

"All the luck," she said.

Then Cole pushed everything but the game out of his mind. After fishing in his jacket pocket, he slipped on a pair of mirror shades and sat down at his designated seat. Taking a quick glance around the table, Cole suspected that none of these guys had ever played in Vegas. They were either online players or avid watchers of poker television tournaments. They looked to be out for a good time and were laughing and joking amongst themselves. The tension in his neck and shoulders eased. This could be a good night.

Poker wasn't gambling. Not to men like him. It was all about statistics and psychology.

Math and science.

Cole glanced up at April, who was nibbling on her lip nervously. He winked at her, but then he realized she couldn't see that through his shades. He felt another pair of eyes on him, and sure enough, on the other side of the room was the man who toasted him before.

The fact that he was on the same level as the poker room, meant he was a player. But he didn't seem to be attached to any games. He was just observing, and for some reason, Cole had caught his attention.

Cole's game started and he forced his attention back to the table.

Eight, three, off suit. Crap on toast. That blew.

Cole folded. It wasn't a good start for the evening. However, it gave him a chance to see what the players in the late betting positions did. That was generally when the more aggressive players bet big. Because Cole didn't have a stake in this pot, he used the time to see if he could figure out what cards each man was holding.

In the next hand, Cole got dealt an ace and a nine, off suit.

Much better. He called, matching the hundred-dollar big blind. The player to his left threw in his cards in disgust. The next player, however, raised the bet, making it cost two hundred and fifty dollars to continue to play. Another player tossed in two hundred and fifty dollars. Everyone else folded.

There was $750 in the pot now. If Cole wanted to see the flop cards, he would have to match the raised bet. He flicked in the chips.

Eight of hearts, nine of hearts and a two of diamonds.

Cole didn't even twitch a smile. Now, he had a pair of nines. The one in his hand and the community card. Because the nine was the highest number in the flop, he had a top pair.

"Check," he said with a bored tone. Let them wonder what he had.

The player two seats down from him raised the bet again to $250.

"Too rich for my blood," the other player said and tossed in his hand.

Cole called and matched the $250.

On the turn card, the nine of spades showed up.

Trip nines.

Three of a kind.

Cole was confident that he had the winning hand.

"Check," he said again, deciding to slow-play it. The other guy was going to lose, but Cole wanted to make sure he wrested every penny out of him first.

The other guy checked.

Cole was disappointed he didn't raise. He wondered what the guy was holding. The only thing that would beat Cole's hand right know was if the other guy had a pair of eights or a pair of twos. That would give the guy a full house. But the man hadn't been betting like he had either of those pairs.

Now, they got to see the river. Four of diamonds.

That card didn't help either of them.

"Five hundred," the other guy called out loudly.

Now, Cole went in for the kill, hoping the man didn't have the pocket eights. "Raise a thousand."

The other guy glared at him, obviously trying to decide if Cole was bluffing. He theatrically played with his chips, then looked at Cole, looked at his cards and played with his chips.

Cole didn't give him so much as a twitch.

Disgusted, the other guy threw in his cards.

The pot was Cole's. He did some quick math in his head. He had made $1400 on that hand—almost two weeks' salary in five minutes. That was a return on investment that even his talented CPA couldn't get him.

Chapter Sixteen

APRIL'S VOICE WAS gone from screaming and cheering. Her makeup had melted off two hours ago and she had a feeling that she looked like a raccoon. She was so exhausted after the all-night poker game, she felt drunk—even though she'd quit drinking at midnight.

"You're a fucking machine," she croaked out. "How are you even still conscious?" April swore she was slurring her words.

"Pure adrenaline," he said, sliding his hand up her bare thigh.

"I almost had a heart attack," she said. "You're like a block of ice."

"Practice makes perfect."

"I still can't believe you won. You won it all. You won a ton," she crowed. Then suddenly it hit her. She grabbed his arm, careful not to yank on it. It was barely six a.m. and there wasn't anyone on the roads yet, but she knew Cole was just as tired as she was. "Cole, don't gamble with your winnings. This was a gift. A fluke."

"This is how I'm going to get my parents out of debt."

She closed her eyes. April didn't have it in her to fight

with him about this. Cole had gone in there with ten thousand dollars—an unimaginable sum, in her mind, to gamble with. He'd left with close to sixty.

"I had been hoping for thirty," Cole said, shaking his head. "Hot damn. I wasn't expecting to double even that. My head is spinning."

"Just wait a bit before paying off bills or hopping into another game. Let's invest some for your future. I make my sisters put away twenty percent for taxes."

"April, the IRS doesn't know I won this money. If we'd been at a casino, they would have taken the taxes out already and sent it in. This was a private game. No one is reporting anything."

She slapped her hands over her ears. "La-la-la. I'm not listening. I didn't hear that. Seriously, though, that's all the more reason to save twenty percent. It's like found money. But you really should claim it on your income taxes." She whispered the last sentence because her conscience made her.

"I've got this. I'm finally back on top."

April knew this was an important conversation, but the hum of the tires on the road was putting her to sleep. She cracked a yawn. "I'm just saying…"

"I know what you're saying. And I love that you're so concerned about me. But I'm good at this. I had forgotten how good."

He *was* good. She thought she was going to be bored, that they would be there for a few hours and then they'd head back to her place after he lost the ten grand. April had it all planned out how she would try to make it up to him with some juicy tidbits off her bucket list, or as she was starting to call it, her sex list. But he played poker like a chess master. She didn't understand the game beyond the basics, but it almost seemed as if Cole had been wearing X-ray glasses instead of mirrored shades.

"Can you read minds?" she asked him sleepily, lulled further into dreamland by the light caress of his hand on her thigh.

"I can remember cards and how people react to good and bad hands. And like I said, I can narrow down what cards they're holding by how and how much they bet."

"Fascinating," she sighed.

The next thing she knew, the car was parked outside of her apartment and Cole was lifting her out.

"Are you going to carry me over the threshold?" she asked.

"I will if you want me to."

She yawned. "I can walk."

He carried her up to the door anyway and set her gently on her feet, then supported her with his big warm body while she fumbled with her keys.

"Cheddar is going to be pissed you kept me out so late," April said.

"I'll get him some catnip to make it up to him."

Finally, she got the door open and stumbled inside. She missed the feel of his body when he didn't follow. "Aren't you coming in?"

"I'd love to," he said reluctantly. "But I've got to get some sleep. I'm working at the Braxton farm again at noon."

"I'm sorry," April said, throwing her arms around him in a big hug.

"Me too. But it's not always going to be this way."

She was happy when he walked her to the bedroom where Cheddar sat on the nightstand, judging her. Cole helped her out of her dress and shoes, then brushed a kiss over each of her nipples.

"I wish I didn't have to work." Tucking her in, he smoothed his hand over her hair. "But you're probably too tired for what I have in mind anyway."

"Rain check?" she murmured, as sleep slowly slipped over her.

"The door's going to lock behind me, right?"

"Mmm hmm."

There was a strange pause and then he said, "Is this your cruise planner?"

"Mmm." Probably. She thought she left it by her bedside.

She heard the sounds of a camera going off, but April was under the covers, so she knew he wasn't taking cheesecake pictures. Then Cole came back to the bed and kissed her sweetly. She didn't even have the energy to lift her arms up to hug him.

THE SOUND OF her phone ringing woke her up at a little past three in the afternoon. She had slept the entire day away.

"Athena!" She bolted upright.

She missed the call, but that was all right. It was her mother reminding her to come to dinner. Right. It was Sunday. She rubbed her face. She saw that there was a text from Cole. She scanned it eagerly, but all it said was that he'd taken care of Athena this morning before going to sleep. She owed him big.

Flopping back into bed, she stared up at the ceiling with a goofy grin on her face. Cole was a saint for remembering to take care of her sister's horse for her. The last thing she wanted June to worry about was Athena. April would have to remember to take some pictures for her sister when she went to feed Athena tonight. After a shower and most of a pot of coffee, April felt ready to face her mother and the third degree. Cheddar wove his way between her ankles.

"I know. I haven't been home much lately," she said, opening a can of wet food for him. When she walked back into her bedroom, she noticed that her cruise planner was open. She remembered Cole's weird question and the sound of him taking pictures. If the spread was anything to go by, he had taken a picture of her flight information and the cruise cabin she had been assigned. What was he up to?

꙳

AFTER A HUGE dinner of meat loaf and mashed potatoes and the third degree about last night, April was feeling sluggish and sleepy. It was going to be an early night for her once she'd mucked out Athena's stall.

But when she got to the stable, the pain in the ass was still out in the pasture. Athena saw her and flicked an ear at her.

"Same to you, Mz. Bitch," she said.

The stall wasn't bad at all, so it was quick work. Once she'd finished and put away the tools, April opened the gate to the pasture to bring Athena in for the night. Closing the gate behind her, she whistled. Athena, of course, pretended that she was deaf. However, the palomino and strawberry roan picked up their heads and headed toward her at an easy pace.

"No, no, no," she muttered, freezing as they approached her.

The palomino tossed her mane as if she was in a shampoo commercial and circled behind her. "S-sunflower?" April said, remembering that this was Emily's horse. Hopefully, Emily would be here soon because Sunflower was standing in front of the gate, waiting to be let into the barn. The other horse was Kelly's. And she was standing way too close to April.

"Okay, P-pippi." April made shooing motions, but Pippi just snorted.

Maybe if she just stayed still, they'd get bored and go away. Or she could be out here for a couple of hours until one of the sisters brought their horses in for the night. This was humiliating.

"I thought you didn't like horses," Cole said.

Moving slowly so as not to startle Pippi, she turned and saw that Cole was carrying a brush and two horse blankets into the corral. "Move, Sunflower," he said gently pushing her aside. He began brushing her, and Pippi moved away, giving April some breathing room, to investigate what he was doing.

"They mobbed me," April said, taking a deep breath.

Athena was paying attention, but still keeping her distance.

"Aren't you supposed to be at work?" she said, still not daring to move.

"I'm through for the evening. But I wanted to take Sunflower and Pippi over to Trent's stable. We're going to use them for barrel lessons tomorrow."

"These two race?" April was shocked. They seemed too laid-back.

"Sunflower is faster and Pippi hasn't done it in a while, but Emily and Kelly used to ride them in Last Stand's rodeo once upon a time." He put the blanket on Sunflower and then turned to brush Pippi. "You could save me a trip and ride Pippi over to the school with me."

"Ride. Me?"

"You said you knew how."

"I haven't been on a horse in years."

"Pippi knows the way to the school. And she won't run unless you want to."

"I don't want to."

"Run or ride."

"Both."

Cole shrugged. "Okay. Be right back. I've got to get the saddles."

He didn't seem disappointed, but April felt a pang of guilt. He'd been so good to her and to Athena. It shouldn't really be a big deal for her to ride up to the school. It would be a fifteen-minute ride tops. And after all, getting more comfortable around horses was something she really wanted to do. April reached a tentative hand to touch Pippi, growing bolder when the mare didn't react.

Cole came back and saddled both horses up. Athena sauntered over and by the time he was finished, she was standing, waiting for her turn.

"Not a chance," April said, giving Athena a wide berth. She got on Pippi's left side. "If you get Athena in the stall, I'll ride Pippi over with you."

"Deal," Cole said. "Are you sure? I don't want you to be afraid."

"It won't be pleasant for me, but if you can vouch for Pippi's manners, I can make it to the school."

"She's a perfect horse for you. Kelly used to ride her bareback. Hell, she would lie on Pippi's back and read a book."

"I will not be doing that. It's a long way down."

Cole walked away then came back with a lead and snapped it on Athena's halter. "Just hold Pippi and Sunflower's leads when I open the gate."

"What if they bolt?" April said, panicking.

"They won't. Stay," he told the horses, looking them in the eyes.

April swallowed hard, but held on to the leads. "Stay," she repeated, trying with all her might not to let her voice shake. Cole opened the gate. Athena lunged forward. Cole's arm muscles bulged as he held her back.

"No. Come when you're called next time and maybe you'll get saddled. Off to bed with you."

Athena dug in.

Cole patiently waited.

It took less time than she would have thought for Athena to give in and allow herself to be put back in her stall. April let out the breath she had been holding. After checking the gate was closed, she dropped the leads and rubbed her arms. She expected the horses to wander off, but they waited like patient soldiers for Cole to come back inside the corral.

"Last chance to chicken out," he said, bringing over a small stepladder so she could climb into the saddle.

"Here goes nothing."

With his help, she got seated astride Pippi with her feet in the stirrups. She was very high off the ground. It took all her concentration not to grip her thighs around Pippi or clutch the reins in terror as Cole led her and Sunflower out of the corral.

"Hold Sunflower, will you?" he said, handing her the reins while he went back to lock the corral.

Now would be the time Athena would take off, leaving her to either follow on a reluctant Raphael or get her arm wrenched out of her socket. April couldn't help tensing up, but neither horse did anything more than take a few steps.

"Thanks," Cole said, hoisting himself into the saddle. "Are you sure that you're all right? I was just teasing you before. I can take both of them in one trip."

"I'm fine," April said, thinking back to the thousand directions her mother and her sisters had shouted at her. Sit up straight. Balance. Watch your lines. Even out your shoulders. Heels under your hips.

"You've got this," Cole said. "You're doing great."

She gave him a tight nod and tried to squash the little squeak that escaped her as the horses started moving. They walked at a slow pace and April tried to relax enough so that each step didn't jar up her tailbone and spine.

The horses knew the way with very little direction. She was glad Cole didn't seem to be interested in talking. She was too busy trying not to make any mistakes. By the time they reached the school, April was starting to get the hang of riding again. She was still intimidated by how high off the ground she was, but Pippi and Sunflower were sweethearts.

Once they were inside the corral, Cole dismounted and helped her off. "Do you feel up to taking care of the tack while I get these two settled?"

"Sure," she said, her legs feeling wobbly.

While Cole walked them around the corral, April filled up their drink buckets and hung them on the hitching posts. Then she helped him take off the saddles and bridles. Cole hosed them down a bit, and they brushed the horses until they were dry and clean. He brought them into their stalls while she put away the equipment and cleaned the area, so it was ready for the students to use tomorrow.

"Good teamwork," he said, giving her a high five. "Can I invite you upstairs for a drink or something?" Cole waggled his eyebrows.

"I'm so damned tempted," she said. "But I'm dead on my feet and I've got a bunch of stuff to do before tomorrow morning to prepare for the week."

"Mondays suck." He nodded.

"Well, they used to. They've gotten better now that I get to see you."

"Maybe next time, we could plan for a Sunday sleepover. You'll love the commute to the office."

"That sounds wonderful," she said.

He interlaced his fingers through hers and walked her back to her car. "You amaze me with how fearless you are."

"Tell that to my sweaty palms," she said. "I'm still shaking inside."

"You faced your fears, and you rode a horse. That's a great first step."

"First step?" She laughed weakly. "This is not going to end up with me barrel racing."

"Three words for you: wild Grayson sister."

"Three words back at you: not gonna happen."

He kissed her. "I'll see you tomorrow."

Chapter Seventeen

MONDAY MORNING CAME way too quickly, but he was in too much of a good mood to spoil it. He'd quit his second job last night. Poker was going to be his second job from now on. That would free up more time for him and April to become even closer. He'd realized that once a week wasn't nearly enough for him. This was the first step in getting serious. Because he had to admit, he was already falling hard and fast for her. Cole fantasized about her all the time—her and her lists.

But the thought of her, alone on that cruise with her damned lists made him wonder if maybe, instead of investing in bonds, he should take a nice long vacation—with her. He deserved it. After confirming the times from her planner the other night, he had checked the cruise's website. The cabin down the hall from her was still available. He was still trying to decide if it would be romantic—or creepy stalkerish—if he showed up unexpectedly, just as they were sailing off. That was the only thing that stopped him from one-clicking it while he was still riding the adrenaline high of his win.

Cole had been about to go down and take care of Athena when he caught sight of Emily riding the horse over. He met her at the corral and let her in.

"June always allowed me and Janice to ride Athena if we wanted to. I figured, if you're going to have a barrel racing demo today, we should see Athena in action."

"Sounds great to me. That mare needs some hard exercise. But make sure none of the kids get near her. From what April tells me, she's surly."

"Aw…" Emily leaned over to pet Athena's mane. "She's just high-strung. She wants to run."

"I'm setting up the course now if you want to do a trial run."

"I've been wanting to do this since we brought her to our place. Janice is going to be so jealous."

Cole got the barrels into the cloverleaf position as Emily trotted around the corral. "Okay, bring her into the alley." He let them out of the corral, so they could go into the rodeo set-up arena that they used for practice.

"You're going to time this, right?" Emily said, her voice high with excitement.

Pulling out a stopwatch from his pocket, he showed it to her. "Fence to fence."

Athena was ready before Emily was, but Emily knew how to ride. The first barrel teetered, but remained up. Athena whirled by the second barrel with a tight spin, and effortlessly circled the third. Thundering back into the alley, Cole clicked his stopwatch. "15:03:69."

"Not bad for a first time. I think she could do better."

"Could Sunflower?"

"Not lately, but she's game to try."

"Looks like Athena wants to go again. We'll do it once more and then cool down."

"Ready whenever you are."

Athena danced over to the start of the alley and then took off with very little direction from Emily. The first barrel seemed to be the hardest, but Emily managed to stop it from tipping over before they sped to the second one. They whipped around the third and came speeding on back.

"This time is14:09:09."

Emily nodded, patting her neck. "Better. I've seen June do low fourteens with her."

"Well, we're not at a rodeo now so time doesn't matter. She sure enjoyed herself."

"I did, too."

"All right, why don't you take care of Athena and give Janice a turn this morning when my class gets here," Cole said.

"If she oversleeps, it's not my fault that someone might have snuck in and turned off her alarm."

Cole plugged his fingers in his ears. "I didn't hear that." Sometimes he was glad he was an only child.

When he got back in the office, April was already there.

"Did you happen to see Emily on Athena?" he asked.

April nodded. "I took a video and some pictures. I'm not sure if June will see them this week or next, but I'm hoping she'll get a kick out of seeing Emily ride hell-bent for leather."

"You should watch the class today."

"I'd like that. It'll be good to get some air."

"I'll try not to show off too much."

"You're good with kids. Ever thought about having some of your own?"

"It's crossed my mind a time or two." Especially lately. "Once things calm down a bit."

Things were going to get better as soon as he won a few more pots. And then he could just go back to having one job and a life that he was hoping April was willing to be a part of. But he didn't want to tie her down. He'd had his chance at running wild. Now, it was her turn.

"I meant to ask you yesterday," she said. "But I was too wound up after riding Pippi. Have you decided what you're going to do with your poker winnings?"

"Half of it is going toward paying off the facility charges for both Mom and Dad's hospital stays. I'll be glad to get that over with."

"Damn, that's a lot of money."

Cole made a face. "It's got to be paid off sooner or later. The other half is for this Friday's game at Donovan's club."

Cole watched April fight to keep herself from saying something.

"It's all their money I'm playing with. I started out with ten thousand."

"So you're going to keep your original stake in the bank? Or invest it and just play with your winnings?"

She'd caught him.

"No, but that's not a bad idea. Maybe I'll do that. You can check in with me next Monday and I'll let you know how it went. This weekend is going to be a no-girls-allowed poker weekend." He leaned a hip on her desk. "Personally? I'm hoping to take them to the cleaners again."

He didn't want to mess with his streak. He needed at least two hundred thousand dollars more to pay everything off. Cole was sick of killing himself working night and day. Not to mention, he couldn't remember when he had bought something or done something that wasn't related to his family.

He could tell she was really upset at the thought of him playing poker with such large sums of money. "Maybe I'll let you convince me to do something productive with my original bet. I hear the stock market is a pretty good way to churn up some cash."

"You're doing this on purpose, aren't you?" She glared at him.

"Only because you're cute when you're angry."

Cole let her swat him because he deserved it. "Here's the thing. It's not like I'm taking the money and blowing it on the slot machines, or craps, or blackjack. Those are all games of chance." He tilted his head. "Maybe you could argue that blackjack can be figured out by card counting, but that depends on how many decks they're using and how often they shuffle."

"It's still gambling," she said.

"Yes, but not the way you're thinking of it. It's not a game of chance like those other casino games are."

"You never know what those community cards are going to be or what two cards the other players are holding or the burn cards that the dealer throws away."

"Not a hundred percent, no. But I can make an educated guess. I've been doing this for years. Think of it like your sisters' rodeo careers. They practice. They train. They put in the time to watch other riders and see what they can do to improve."

"But it's not foolproof. In the end, sometimes it all comes down to the horse having a bad day."

"Exactly. Sometimes you win. Sometimes you lose. But it's like that with everything."

"Okay, but if my sisters come in last, they haven't lost a year's salary."

He got her.

"Haven't they?" He saw the revelation come slowly over her face. "If they don't win, they don't get sponsors. If they don't rank high enough, they can't compete at the higher levels. If they don't put on a show, they don't keep their fans interested."

"I can see your point. It just makes my head spin, the risks you take. You need to play it safer."

"I tell you what. You take a few more risks and I'll play it a little safer. We can meet in the middle. Sound good?"

"I think so," she said.

"Okay, beautiful, I've got to get to work."

She stood up and walked him to the door. "Sounds like you're going to be busy this week. I was hoping to see if we could squeeze in some personal time."

"I wish you could come by the game and be my good luck charm again this weekend, but it's guys only—those are the rules."

"I wouldn't want to get my girl cooties all over your chips."

"I like your girl cooties." He drew her into his arms. He hadn't had his good-morning kiss yet. Her lips parted for him as he held her tight. What on earth was he going to do when he couldn't kiss her like this every morning? Maybe he could convince Trent that he needed a full-time accountant, because Cole certainly needed her with him twenty-four, seven.

At the sound of footsteps in the hallway, they sprang apart. If Trent had noticed that Cole was studying the wall intently, he didn't mention it.

"April, can I ask you a favor?" Trent said.

"Of course."

"Kelly isn't feeling too well today. Everything's fine," he rushed to add. "She's just a little stomach sick. I was wondering if I could impose on you to help my mother-in-law out in the kitchen. She's cooking lunch for the ranch hands and she'll need some help setting up by the pasture they're working on today."

"I don't have to ride a horse, do I?"

Trent chuckled. "No, just an old pickup. It shouldn't take more than a couple hours and you get a free lunch out of it. I'll pay you for your time."

"That's not necessary. I'd be glad to help you guys out. You've been great about taking in my sister's horse and treating her like your own." She grabbed her purse. "Should I go over there now?"

"If you would, that would be a load off my mind."

"I'm on it."

Cole walked her out. "Well, damn. I was hoping to convince you to take a long lunch with me up in my bedroom today."

"How about tomorrow?" She leaned in close. "Now that I know in advance, I can wear some sexy lingerie."

"How sexy are we talking about?"

"Let's just say there's a little bit of leather and a little bit of lace."

"Doesn't sound very comfortable."

"It's not meant to be on for very long." April kissed him on his neck, lingering to nibble and suck.

"Darlin', you're about to have truck sex again if you keep that up."

"Sure, with half the ranch looking on." She darted away from his groping hands.

"I'll see you later." He grabbed her for another kiss because it felt right.

Cole couldn't give her the relationship that she deserved—not yet anyway. But with each poker game, he was getting closer.

Chapter Eighteen

APRIL WOUND UP staying at the ranch house with Sarah so Kelly could rest. She played checkers with Alissa and got beaten badly by the six-year-old. After helping Sarah with dinner, she declined to stay and eat with the family, mostly because Emily and her father were butting heads over the treatment of the cattle, but also because she wanted to bring Cole over some dinner and maybe go skinny-dipping again.

After taking care of Athena for the night, April was all horsed out. She went back home and took a quick shower, then packed an overnight bag with a change of clothes and a big towel. It paid to be prepared.

On the way out to the Braxtons' farm, she stopped at the deli and picked up some sandwiches, a couple of bottles of root beer, and a bag of chips. She stifled a yawn and the urge to close her eyes just for a moment while the cashier rang up the items. It had been tiring out there in the hot sun today. April was glad she wasn't a cowboy.

All those horses aside, it was tough work. But the horses were still a problem for her. She had thought after riding Pippi that she would miraculously have gotten over her fear.

But when she'd had to walk by them this afternoon, all of them clustered together in one place, she'd almost dropped the pitchers of sweet tea she was carrying.

Luckily, Nate had been there to save the tea before she dropped it. She could tell that he didn't have any use for someone who didn't see horses as a part of their lives, so April stayed out of his way, standing behind the table and making sure all the ranch hands were well fed and hydrated, while Sarah handled anything horse-related. So much for progress…

When April pulled into the farm, Mr. Braxton came out to greet her.

"Cole's not here," he said, looking at her and her picnic basket curiously.

"He's not?" She was pretty sure that she didn't see his truck outside of the school when she drove past it. "Is everything all right?"

Braxton shrugged. "I guess so. He quit on me. I can't say I'm surprised. That boy was running himself ragged."

"Quit?"

"He said he didn't need the part-time work anymore. I'm sorry to lose him—he was a hard worker."

April was confused. Where could he be? Was he involved with another poker game?

"He's probably at his parents' house, if you're looking for him."

"Am I that easy to read?" she said.

"Let's just say, you shouldn't play poker."

April gave a noncommittal grunt. She thought of someone else who shouldn't be playing poker, either. "Thanks."

Before she could think it through, she decided to drive past the Lockwood farm. April half-remembered some gossip about the pastures being sold off. That would mean that the property was basically just the house and a garden now.

Sure enough, Cole's truck was there, along with another car. She parked behind the truck and sat there thinking. Her mama would be appalled if she showed up unannounced and they were having dinner or a get-together of some sort. On the other hand, she had wanted to surprise Cole with a picnic. Only she hadn't brought enough for his parents. She wasn't even sure if they were on a restricted diet. She should probably go. She had to practice her dancing and Cheddar had been missing her lately.

And yet, the wild Grayson sister in her urged her to just go up to the door and knock. If she was interrupting something, she'd apologize and leave. Compromising, she pulled out her phone and texted Cole, asking him what he was doing.

She heard his incoming text tone faintly. It was coming from his truck. Blowing out an aggravated sigh, she got out of the car. She was glad he'd quit his second job, because he'd been working himself ragged. But April was afraid that he'd let his false confidence in his poker game get the better of him. He was good. Amazingly good. But there was always someone better.

Ringing the doorbell, she admired the house. While it had seen better days, it still made an impression. It was large, just short of being a mansion, in her opinion. They could have fit her mama's trailer and Tulip's pen in the first floor alone. Craning her neck to look up, she saw there were three floors. Cole had said he was an only child. What did three people do with all this space?

Cole opened the door and did a double take.

"If you're busy, I can leave." April showed him the picnic basket. "I stopped by Braxtons' to see if you were up for dinner and skinny-dipping again, but he said you had quit." She raised her eyebrow at him.

He darted a glance behind him. "I have to stick around here in case my parents need me. It's Gwen's night off. She's the home healthcare aide."

"I don't want to barge in," she said. Was she being too needy?

"Not at all. I'd love the company."

"Are you sure? I didn't bring enough for your parents. But I could go back out and get something else." She backed down the stairs.

"No, that's all right. They already ate. Come on in. I'll give you the grand tour."

Still feeling a little self-conscious, April handed him the basket and took his offered hand to help her up the stairs. They walked into the foyer and April gaped.

"Wow, look at all this marble. I bet it's hell to keep clean with all the mud that gets tracked in."

"We don't come in this way usually. There's a mudroom in the back off the garage." He pointed. "My parents' rooms are off the parlor. The dining room and kitchen are over here."

The kitchen looked commercial, large, and industrious. "My mama would live in this room alone," April said, running her fingers over the stainless-steel countertops. But as big as it was, it lacked the warmth of the trailer's kitchen. It could use a few kitschy hand towels.

"Are you expecting the Last Stand baseball team to have dinner?" she joked when they went into the living room. A large oak table and chairs were centered in the room, overlooked by a large glass chandelier.

"My parents loved to entertain. They don't get much chance to nowadays."

April immediately felt bad. "Of course. I'm sorry."

"It's okay. It is what it is."

The parlor was a gorgeous room with two large couches, a recliner, and a large-screen television. The carpet was white plush, and the furniture was accented with gold and brown. Again, April marveled at how pristine it all was for a rancher's house in a dusty Texas town.

"I think my parents are in their room resting, otherwise I'd introduce you. They basically moved their bedroom from upstairs to down here, so they didn't have to navigate the stairs."

"That must have been expensive."

Cole nodded. "I helped do some of the work, but yeah, it was. It was worth it, though because I don't have to worry about them falling."

Though the stairs were wide with a sturdy railing, April would have been worried about her own mama navigating them if she was sick.

"What's upstairs?"

"Bedrooms, my parents' offices, the library and the music room."

"It's like a Clue game in here. Billy Bob killed Ms. Maple in the music room with the pitchfork."

Cole laughed self-consciously.

"What about the third floor?"

"Attic and storage. The parlor used to be my dad's man cave, so the pool table and bar are up there now."

"Is it set up? My sisters taught me how to hustle a game of pool. My skills are rusty."

"You're on. But it's hot as hell up there. Let me put on the air conditioner first and then we can go eat. By the time we're done, it should be cool enough for us to play and have a few drinks."

"You mean like a real date?" she said.

"I'm not sure if it counts if it's in my parents' house, but close enough."

She followed him up to the third floor. It was hot, but not uncomfortably so. Still, after the day she'd had, she'd be tempted to fall asleep if she had to sit up here for long without the air on. Cole turned the A/C up so the room would cool down to a more reasonable temperature and then led her downstairs and out on the patio.

"You thought of everything," he said as she laid out the food.

"I'm surprised there's no pool," she said, waving her hand at the wide expanse of the backyard garden.

"My parents aren't much for swimming."

"Too bad," she said, running her foot up his calf. "I had plans for tonight."

"Maybe we could modify them?" He tucked a hair behind her ear and leaned over the table to kiss her. "This was a nice surprise."

"Speaking of surprises, why didn't you tell me why you were quitting your second job? You're still staying with Trent, right?"

"Of course. I love working with the kids. Quitting my second job was a sudden decision."

"Don't get me wrong, I'm glad that you did. It was only a matter of time before working so many hours was going to affect your health." She unwrapped his sandwich and handed it to him. "I'm just worried you're putting too much pressure on yourself to win at poker. I got the impression that the people you were playing with had money to burn. Couldn't they just out-bet you until you ran out of money?"

"They could. But I tend to fold if I see that happen. I let the other players get caught in that trap. And if they go all in and I can't match, as long as I know I'm going to win, I don't mind pushing in what I've got."

"That's the fuzzy part for me. How do you know you're going to win?"

"Like I said, it's all about reading the players and observing how they bet in all their positions. I really wish you could watch again Friday night. I think you'd see the logic behind it."

"Do you think I'll understand it better if I watched a few YouTube videos?" April was still unconvinced, but she'd seen him in action, and he knew what he was talking about.

"It couldn't hurt. How did everything go today with Sarah?"

April got the feeling that he was deliberately changing the subject, but she let him. Besides, she couldn't argue that he would be able to pay off a significant chunk of medical bills with his winnings, but the risks he was taking made her feel faint. Looking up at the house, though, she thought again that selling it and moving his parents into a smaller place was a smarter move. Then again, she hadn't grown up in a place like this. Maybe she'd feel differently if she'd ever lived in a mansion.

After their quick picnic, Cole cleaned up the mess. "The third floor should be bearable now."

It was much cooler and April eagerly went over to the pool table and started collecting the billiard balls to put into the triangle form in the center of the green felt.

"Can I get you something to drink?" he asked from behind the fully stocked bar.

"Jack and Coke," she said. After the balls were racked perfectly, she took off the triangle and set it aside. "What was in storage up here that took up all this room?"

"Trunks from all of our ancestors, going back to the earliest days of Last Stand. When we had to move the man cave up here, we donated most of the stuff to the Keeping Society." Cole looked around. "We donated a lot. My mom was sorry to see it go. She used to love to come up here and sort through things, spending hours looking at all the pictures of the past and reading the journals that her great-great-someone or another had written. But we couldn't have her walking up all the stairs and it was too cost-prohibitive to put in an elevator."

April couldn't even imagine a residence with an elevator that wasn't an apartment building or condo.

"So the library was nice enough to set up a corner for the collection and she's got VIP treatment with her own chair and table whenever she wants to visit it. She hasn't really felt up to it lately, though."

"This is a lot of house for just the two of them. If you moved back in, you could have the second floor and this one all to yourself."

"But it would be a little awkward trying to sneak you in and out, without them noticing."

"Why would we have to sneak?" April said, crossing her arms. "We're adults."

"Don't you think it's a little awkward? How would you feel if you had to walk me past your mother when we were going to your bedroom?"

April snorted. "Good point. It would be twenty questions and then I'd be too self-conscious to enjoy having you there. Still, it seems like such a waste of a good house."

Cole handed her the drink he'd just made. "Well, let's not waste it."

Clinking glasses with him, she took a sip. "Will we disturb your parents if we put on some music?"

"Not if we keep it low." He fiddled with the sound system and soon, Garth Brooks was singing about two piña coladas.

"Okay, let's see what you got." April handed him a pool cue and indicated he should break.

They were pretty evenly matched and were starting their second game when the intercom system cut off the music. "Cole? Can you come down here? Dad needs some help."

"Be right back," Cole said, setting his cue down.

April walked around the room, taking in the framed newspaper articles of Cole's father with various politicians and some celebrities. There was a rodeo trophy that Cole had won in high school in the trophy case and a few other medals and ribbons. She could see how hard it would be to give this all up and move to a smaller place. But she still thought it was better than counting on his poker winnings to make ends meet.

Taking out her phone, she started to do some research on how much they could expect to sell a house like this in today's market. She was so engrossed with the numbers that she didn't hear Cole come back.

"Sorry it took so long," he said. "What are you looking at so intently?"

She was so startled that the phone toppled out of her hand. Cole managed to catch it before it hit the floor. He glanced at it and his lips tightened. "It's not going to happen. Put it out of your mind."

April held up her hands in surrender. "I was just curious. You wanted me to come over and take a look at your taxes and finances. I'm just doing my fiduciary duty and exploring all options for you."

His eyes narrowed. "That sounds like a fancy way of saying you were snooping."

"It's not. But I was curious, that's all. Do you want me to take a look at the financial records now?" April said, her stomach a little queasy at his accusations.

"Well, that's not exactly how I planned the end of this date to go, but since you're in that frame of mind, you might as well. The office is on the second floor." He tanked the rest of his drink and shut off the music.

Great. Accountant April had come back with a vengeance.

Chapter Nineteen

COLE HAD BEEN looking forward to Friday night all week. Unfortunately, things had been tense between April and him ever since he'd let her look at the finances. He didn't know why he was so ashamed of the mess they were in. It wasn't his fault. It wasn't anyone's fault. And while he could have been better with money during his poker days, he had learned a hell of a lot about himself since then. Poker was now his second job. Before it had been a way to avoid adult responsibilities, but now it was a way to dig his family out of the hole that all the medical bills had put them in. He had been as wild as April claimed her sisters were. It had been a hell of a ride, and he had paid for the good times. Now, he just needed a few more winning pots to give his family some breathing room.

April did have some great ideas about using the historical donations as tax deductions and agreed to help him get the proper documentation. She was even researching the best ways to deduct some of the medical expenses. But he wouldn't consider selling the house.

"You've put a lot of work into this place and I know it means a lot to you. But your solution to the medical bills is right here," she had said. "In this market, you could sell it and pay off all the bills, and even have enough left over for your parents to live on."

"Where would they stay? This is their home. It's been in the family for generations."

"They could stay wherever they want."

"They're too old to move," he had said.

"Have you asked them?"

Cole didn't even know how to broach the subject with his parents. But one thing he was certain about—he wanted April in his life. But before he could take the next step, he needed to make sure he wouldn't be a financial burden to her. That didn't mean they couldn't start dating like a normal couple, though.

First, he had to get this poker game behind him.

He stopped by the barn where April was taking care of Athena before he headed over to the game. She was just finishing up.

"Hey, good-looking," he said. She had hay in her hair and mud on her face. He still leaned in to kiss her. It was their first kiss this week.

Shrieking, she jumped back. "I'm filthy."

"I don't care."

"Cole, you're wearing a white shirt and you smell better than I do."

"So what?"

"So, nothing." April shooed him away.

"I just wanted a good-luck kiss."

She blew him one. "You don't need luck, remember?"

"Everyone needs a little luck. Can I call you later?"

"Why don't you call me tomorrow when it's all over?"

"I'll make a deal with you. I'll take care of Athena tomorrow morning and then we can go out for breakfast."

She bit her luscious lip and Cole wanted to back her into the barn for some more lip biting. "How about I make you breakfast, and we stay in for the day?" she said. "Unless you have to work?"

Cole shook his head. "I gave up everything but my day job. I'm all yours this weekend."

Taking a deep breath, she asked, "How about beyond this weekend?"

Delight and desire warred within him. "Why, Wild April Grayson, are you asking me to be your boyfriend?"

Setting her jaw, she nodded. "I am."

Cole had been going to ask her tomorrow, after the poker game, but he supposed there was no time like the present. He gave her a courtly bow. "I humbly accept." He was glad they were on the same page.

She grinned at his antics. "I was hoping you would say that."

"You beat me to it. Now that I can have some kind of social life, I'm more than anxious to share my time with you."

"How do you feel about naked pancakes, then?" April said.

"I can't wait." He wished he could take her up on her offer right now. It was difficult to pull himself away from the barn. "I'll see you soon."

"Cole," she said, following him out with a concerned frown on her face. "It doesn't matter to me if you win or lose tonight. I'm all in either way."

He grinned at her poker reference. "I'm all in, too."

Walking down to Donovan's club, Cole had to pass by Janice's retreat. He was surprised to find the man he'd seen at the country club having a smoke outside.

"You following me?" Cole asked.

The man pitched his cigarette and approached him. Holding out his hand, he said, "I'm Charlie Lincoln. I rent the wellness retreat a couple of times a year for my group. I recognized you from around the ranch. I was going to introduce myself last week in San Antonio, but I didn't want to interrupt your winning streak. You play a mean game of poker."

"Thanks," Cole said. "Are you playing tonight?"

Charlie shook his head. "No. The owner of the hunting club and I have had differences in the past. But I'd be interested in any other venue. I was too late getting into a game at the country club, but I sure enjoyed watching. You never know what you can pick up."

Charlie didn't seem to be a high roller, but then again, neither did Cole. "Give me your number and I'll put you in touch with my guy, Vic. He arranges for all sorts of games in this area. He's a good guy."

"I appreciate that. Hope you get the big full tonight." Charlie handed him a business card with his name and number on it.

"Wouldn't that be nice?" Cole tucked it in his shirt

pocket. "You have a good night."

"I'll try." Charlie looked longingly down the road to the hunting lodge and then with a nod, turned around and headed back into the retreat.

Cole continued walking down the trail to Donovan's hunting lodge. He didn't need three aces and two kings to win. He'd be happy with just having the higher card full house, if it came down to it. In fact, as long as his hole cards weren't twos and sevens, he'd be okay.

He saw a few familiar faces from San Antonio, but it was mostly a new crew. They were talking about hunting feral hogs tomorrow and Cole was glad they were going to make a weekend out of it.

After settling up with Vic, who was charging his usual five hundred dollars from each player as a finders' fee for the game, he passed on Charlie Lincoln's information as a possible player.

"I don't know much about the guy, but he seems to know his game." Cole caught Donovan's eye and waved him over.

"Good crowd. I'm looking forward to watching because the buy-in is too rich for my blood. You guys don't mind an audience, do you? Nate and I are looking to pick up some pointers," Donovan said.

"Not at all. I'm just happy we could have a game here." Cole accepted a bottle of beer from him. He'd swap it out with water just before they started the game. He didn't want anything clouding his head. "Say, what can you tell me about Charlie Lincoln?"

Donovan's entire body stiffened. "He's an ex-con and a grifter. I wouldn't give him a dime of my money or trust him with anything important. You can always tell when he's lying though. His mouth is open."

"That bad, huh?" Cole and Vic exchanged a significant look. Vic crumpled the card and tossed it in the trash.

"Has he been bothering you?" Donovan said. "I'll file a complaint with Janice, and she can get his parole officer on his case."

"No, not at all. I was just talking with him. He was out having a smoke when I passed by." Cole was pretty sure it was a parole violation to gamble and he didn't want to get the man in trouble.

Donovan grunted. "Well, you let me know."

"I didn't mean to ruin his night," Cole said to Vic as Donovan stormed away.

"Don't worry about him. Worry about these guys. The two that you took to the cleaners last week are out for your blood. They want a chance to get their money back."

"I don't know. If they play like they did last week, I can't see that happening."

"Don't get cocky. You never know when Lady Luck is going to kick you to the curb."

🎏

APRIL DIDN'T WANT to spend Friday night alone. But the sweet shock of being able to call Cole her boyfriend made it bearable. Cheddar jumped up on her lap, scattering her multi-colored pens and sticky notes all over the floor. But she couldn't scold him. He was just looking for attention. She tickled him under the chin and stroked her hand down his soft back and up his fluffy tail. Putting on their favorite TV show, she settled in for the night. Sometimes it was good to be boring April.

When her phone rang, waking her, April wasn't sure what time it was. She must have fallen asleep because Netflix wanted to know if she was still watching. Clicking no, she answered her phone.

"Hello?"

"Great! You're still up!"

"Cole, what time is it?" It was still dark out. His voice was as rough as sandpaper, but there was a manic joy in it that did weird things to her stomach.

"The game just broke up. I won, baby. Again. I won it all."

Shock plastered her to the couch. "How much?"

"Sixty thousand dollars. Again."

"Cole, you did it. This is amazing. Congratulations." April didn't want to rain on his parade. He had done the impossible. At least, impossible for her. She didn't want him to think this was normal, but what if it was? After that night at the country club, she'd done some research on professional poker players. They *did* make a living out of playing a game. But she knew better than most that nothing was a sure thing. Even this latest venture of hers, being her own boss, spiked her anxiety up to eleven sometimes when she thought of the money drying up.

"I've got a question for you. And I want you to answer honestly," he said.

"Are you on your way here?" She popped up, spilling Cheddar off her lap. She wasn't going to think about money. Not yet, anyway. Cole deserved to celebrate. But damn, she needed to pick up a few things. Maybe vacuum and do dishes. Brush her teeth. She licked across her teeth. That first.

"Is that okay?"

"Of course. Ask me the question when you get here."

"See you soon."

April darted around the apartment like a madwoman, picking things up. She finished up in the bathroom, with a lightning-quick shower and a gargle of mouthwash. She was fighting with the complicated underwear she had bought at a sexy boutique when the doorbell rang.

"Shit," she said, grabbing the flimsy robe. She shrugged it on and pulled the thong out of the crack of her butt. Striking a pose, she opened the door, hoping belatedly that it was Cole and not the UPS guy.

Thankfully, it was Cole who caught her up in his arms and swung her around. She could see the first rays of dawn lighting the sky before he closed the door with his boot heel. Then his mouth was crushing hers, his whiskers driving her crazy. When he was unshaven, he looked like the bad boy she used to know.

Their tongues played with each other, and Cole groaned into her mouth. He slid his hand down her body to cup her ass and pull her against his hardness. Would she ever get enough of him? Now on fire, April greedily unbuttoned his shirt, while he backed her into the bedroom.

When they reached the bed, she reluctantly broke away from his magical kisses. Eagerly, she pressed her mouth down his chest, to the hard muscles of his abdomen. Kneeling now, April unbuttoned his jeans and pulled them and his underwear down.

She licked up the long, hard length of him while his fingers tangled in her hair.

"What are you wearing?" His eyes were half closed.

"These old things?" April took him into her mouth.

Cole swayed. "Damn."

She swirled her tongue around him. Gripping his shaft tight, she slowly took him in and out of her mouth. He held her head still and rocked against her.

"That feels so damned good. I want you so much. I need to touch you. Come up here." He guided her head back until his cock slid out of her mouth with a loud pop.

April licked him again, but didn't move. Bending down, Cole picked her up and tossed her on the bed. She landed with a laughing shriek and a bounce. Cole pulled off his boots and kicked out of his pants and then he was naked in her bed. He was so gorgeous, he made her mouth water. He tossed a condom on the night table.

"These are pretty," he said tracing her nipples through the thin silk.

He kissed her again while he rubbed between her legs. His fingers were skilled and before she knew it, April was gasping her orgasm into his mouth. Her fingernails dug into his shoulders when he went from torturing her clit to thrusting his fingers inside her. But it wasn't enough. She wanted more.

"Cole," she whispered, her lips feeling swollen and pouty. "Fuck me."

He rolled them both over so he was on his back and grabbed the condom. She went back to sucking on him while he fumbled to get the package open.

"If you don't stop, I'm going to come in your mouth instead of your sweet pussy."

April took that as a dare and went faster, loving the taste of his silky hardness.

"April, baby." Cole bucked and gasped. His fingers gripped her hair, the condom forgotten on his chest. She hummed in pleasure when his other hand caressed up and down her back.

She sucked until he tensed, and with an inarticulate grunt came down her throat. Easing him out of her mouth, she unrolled the condom on his still hard cock.

"I changed my mind. I'm going to fuck you instead," she said. And grinning, she moved to sit astride him.

Pushing the thong to the side, Cole guided himself inside her. The pleasure of feeling him slowly slide into her, made her weak. She clung to his chest until she sat fully on top of him.

"Oh my," she panted. "That's so damned good."

"Took the words out of my mouth." Cole's voice was husky. He gently tugged off the robe and pulled on the scraps of silk that covered her breasts. Freeing them, he bent to suck on her nipples. When his hot tongue flicked across them, her entire body clenched. April rode him desperately, holding his head to her this time.

"Yes," she cried out over and over again as she bounced on him.

Pleasure and joy zinged through her and she shook apart as he held her tight. The next thing she knew, he had her on her hands and knees, and was sinking deep inside her. She clamped hard around him, her fingers gripping the bed-covers.

He took her so hard and fast, she screamed as another electrical wave of bliss hit her. He rode her through it and just when she thought he was going to finish, he flipped her on her back. Cole held her wrists above her head and thrust into her slowly, staring into her eyes.

The intensity was almost too much, but she couldn't look away.

"I need to ask you something," he said, his eyes clouded with lazy desire.

"Anything," April said, breathlessly. "Just don't stop." Her nerves were finely tuned to a fever pitch and she was so close to exploding into a puddle of exhausted contentment.

"Let me go on the cruise with you."

Reason fled and she arched into his thrusts. "Yes. Yes. Oh yes." It wasn't the fiscally responsible thing to do and it didn't align with her goals of being independent, but it would ratchet the fun factor into the atmosphere to share her European cruise with someone she loved.

Wait.

Loved?

She choked on the realization as she came uncontrollably around him. She felt as if she was flying, that her life was finally taking off in the direction she wanted it to go. And if the voice of reason was trying to get a word in edgewise, April was deliberately going to turn a deaf ear. She'd been a good girl for long enough.

Chapter Twenty

COLE HAD HATED going back to the hunting lodge on Saturday morning and spending the weekend with Donovan's guests. He'd managed not to lose the money he had won and even got to do some hunting on Saturday. But the best part of the weekend had been when April had packed an overnight bag and stayed Sunday night at his place. He loved waking up with her in his arms. The time he'd spent with her this past month was the best in his life.

"I could get used to this commute," she said, happily lounging next to him when his alarm went off. "It makes Mondays so much better."

"You make Mondays better," he said, kissing the top of her head. He knew he had to get in the shower or they were both going to be late for work.

They decided to shower together to save time, but they still walked down about fifteen minutes late. Of course, Trent was already there and had opened the school. Trent called him over as soon as he saw him.

"Busted," April singsonged and sidled past him into their office. Cole would have swatted her on the butt, but Trent was looking right at him with a frown on his face.

"I'm sorry I'm late, boss," Cole said.

"Huh? Oh, were you?" Trent motioned him into his office. "It's no problem. I'm a little distracted. Kelly had a rough weekend. The baby is making her sick and I'm a little worried about her."

"Did she see a doctor about it?" Cole hoped there was nothing wrong. Kelly and Trent had had a rocky start and they deserved to have a smooth path from now on.

"The doctor said she and the baby are just fine. But I don't feel right about leaving her alone right now."

Cole nodded. "I can do whatever you need done."

"Well, I'm scheduled to go to Vegas this week. The Odyssey casino is hosting a rodeo and a stockyard. I got comped a hotel and ticket to the event. I was going to go and take a look at some bulls, but like I said, I don't feel right about leaving Kelly. Would you mind going and taking notes on what's being offered? I can send you as my liaison."

Cole couldn't believe what he was hearing. A free trip to Vegas? He had been going to pay off another few bills after booking the cruise, but this was even better. He could double his money and it would be like taking the cruise for free. He smiled, thinking what April would think of that logic.

"Take April, if you want. It will be a nice getaway."

"April?" Cole said.

"I'm distracted, not blind." Trent snorted.

"I'd love to go. Vegas is one of my favorite cities." Lady Luck had definitely been in his corner lately.

"Great. Grab us some coffee. We've got time before the

first class comes in. I want to bring you up to speed on what I'm looking to buy."

WHEN APRIL FOUND out she was going to Vegas for a rodeo, her first call was to Merry. Because, of course, she was on the schedule. And naturally, Merry's first thought was who was going to take care of Athena.

"Emily said she would do it," April said, rolling her eyes.

"You should offer to pay her. This is their business. We don't need a handout."

"It's not like that," April argued.

But Merry was adamant. "It'll be about a hundred bucks for the weekend. I'll pay it if you don't."

"I'll take care of it," April said, trying not to be annoyed at her sister. Merry was too proud for her own good. She could never accept a gift without looking for ulterior motives. Someone must have burned her badly when they were younger, but April didn't know who. But she would have kicked that person's ass if she did. "Have you heard from June?"

"She's allowed one phone call a week. You'd be better off asking Mama."

"Sounds like jail," April said, frowning at her computer. "What about email?"

"Nope. No computers. Nothing that could swap one addiction for another. You can mail her a letter though. She'll be in there for another two months."

"I hate to think of her there."

"She's getting the help she needs."

"Maybe I'll send her a postcard from Vegas." Or would that make things worse?

Merry grunted. "So...Cole Lockwood, huh? Isn't he the bulldogger you had a crush on in high school?"

"The very same."

"It's serious?"

"I'm going to Vegas with him, aren't I?" April retorted.

"You're not going to get married by Elvis, are you?"

"Of course not!" But what a cool idea. "We just started dating. It's too early for that."

"Well, if he doesn't treat you right, I'm going to tie him to the back of my horse and drag him all over that ranch."

"That's sweet. I'll make sure to let him know."

"I'll tell him myself."

"Please don't scare him off. I really like him."

"If he really liked you, I wouldn't be able to scare him off."

"Merry," April said warningly.

"Fine," Merry said grudgingly. "But just keep your eye on him. He comes from money. His family throws charity balls for people like us."

April was shaking her head at her sister's paranoia. "They do not."

"He strikes me as the type who has a tuxedo in his closet for any last-minute plans."

April thought back to her first glimpse of Cole, walking into the Bluebonnet Country Club like he owned the place.

"Well, that part is true. And he looks damned good in it."

Merry whistled. "Just be careful. You've got no experience with cowboys like that."

"Well I was inexperienced, but I've been broadening my horizons."

"Good for you. I'll see you when you get here. I'll email you and Mr. Tuxedo passes to allow you access to the arena level where the chutes are."

"Thanks," April said. "I can't wait to see you this weekend."

It was going to be weird, seeing Merry at a rodeo and not being put to work as part of the crew. April was going to have to make sure she didn't fall into old habits. Merry had been taking care of her own horse and keeping herself hydrated between matches for several years now. While there was something exciting about being part of a winning team, April was having too much fun being the star attraction of Cole's world to ever want to go back to being in the background.

That didn't mean she wasn't supportive of her sister. She just didn't know where she stood in this new world where she was the wild Grayson sister with a handsome lover and an exciting sex life.

Chapter Twenty-One

THE VEGAS ADVENTURE started with joining the mile high club, which sounded better on paper than in reality. But Cole was willing to do anything to help April finish up her list. The flight was three hours in length, but timing was crucial. They had to wait for the captain to turn off the seat belt sign, and then, make sure the flight attendants were busy with beverage service.

And finally, then they had to casually monitor the bathrooms, making sure one was free, with no one in line waiting. April had researched this thoroughly. They even practiced in the rodeo's school's bathroom instead of going upstairs to Cole's apartment. But the timing was hard to gauge, because everyone came and went at their leisure. They almost got caught by Alissa. Luckily, she had been too distracted looking for her daddy to see them adjusting their clothes.

As the plane leveled off and the foot traffic to the bathroom disappeared, April gave him the nod. Cole went in first and a few seconds later, April joined him. She was giggling, but she was prepared.

"I bought lube and a condom, just in case," she said,

handing him both.

"I am in awe of you. Your planning skills are mind-boggling, do you know that?"

"I try." April pulled the baby-changing table down over the toilet and spread the scarf that she had been wearing around her neck down on top of it. "Hoist me up and slip off my panties."

It should have been ridiculous, and not erotic, but he got hard as he did what she asked.

Placing her legs on the wall to either side of him, he realized that this was going to happen. Never in a million years had he contemplating having sex in an airplane bathroom.

"Put the condom on," she said.

"I'm going to need a little help."

"I can't reach you."

"Can you reach yourself?" He unzipped his pants and took his cock out.

She stared at him, all hungry eyes and innocence. He couldn't believe this beautiful woman was so into him. Pulling up her dress, she put her hands between her thighs.

"That's right," he whispered, stroking himself. "Let me see you get off."

The plane rumbled and dipped, but they were crammed in so tight they barely moved.

"Faster baby," he said. "It'll be quick now, but I'll go nice and slow when we get to the hotel. I'm going to make you ride my face until you come all over it."

"Oh," she said and quivered.

He was rock hard. "Do you want some lube?"

She nodded.

Slipping on the condom, he poured some on. "Now?" he asked.

"Yeah," she said huskily.

It was easier once he was inside her. Trying not to make too much noise or bang around was the hard part. She went wild.

"You're crazy," he said against her mouth.

"You're with me," she said. "So who's the crazy one?"

She was so hot and tight, he never wanted to stop, but he was well aware they were pressing their luck. "What can I do to make you come?"

"I'm so close," she said, writhing on him. "Talk dirty to me."

He rocked into her rhythmically. "When we get to the hotel, I'm going to have to practice my poker game before I find one. We're going to play strip poker and when you're naked, we're going to play for sex acts instead of chips."

She shuddered and her breathing picked up.

"I'd have you blow me in the elevators, but there are cameras everywhere." He thrust hard and she covered her mouth when she shrieked.

"I want to see you pole dance for me."

"Too bad I left the pole at home," she muttered, her fingernails digging into him. She arched into his thrusts and moaned low in her throat.

"We're about to touch down in the city of sin," he said. "I can rent a stripper pole, and have it installed in our hotel room before we land."

April thrust back at him just as hard and he had to lock himself down tight before he came too quickly. She had to come first.

"I'll do anything you want, card game or no."

That nearly sent him over the edge.

Baseball.

Taxes.

Clenching his jaw, Cole pumped into her in quick jerky strokes. When her eyes crossed, he knew she was close. "I'm going to take you on our balcony during the cruise. I want you holding the railing and staring off into the ocean when you come."

Bingo.

She convulsed and tightened her sweet pussy around him. He rode out her contractions before coming quickly behind her.

"I don't think I can move my legs," she said.

"Give me a sec and I'll help." He cleaned himself up as much as possible and buttoned up his pants. Easing her panties back on, he lifted her up and secured the baby-changing tray. Her legs slowly hit the floor. She balled up the scarf and put it in the trash.

"Okay, you go first. I'll be right out."

Nodding, Cole carefully eased out of the bathroom and closed it behind him. They were in luck. No one was waiting for the bathroom, but one of the flight attendants gave him an arch look. He made his way back to his seat, his legs feeling like jelly.

APRIL HAD FORGOTTEN how much she missed the rodeo. And with her cowboy holding her hand as they made their way to where the riders were gathering around the chutes in the backstage area of the arena, she could almost ignore the presence of all the horses.

Merry saw her first and grabbed her in a hug that tore her away from Cole, who watched in amusement. Merry had lightened her dark hair to a honey blond and wore a Stetson that was both sexy and intimidating. She looked professional and ready to kick some ass.

"You are going to do great," April said returning the fierce hug.

"It's good to see you. I didn't think I would until Emily's bachelorette party." Merry speared Cole with a defiant look. "Lockwood."

"Grayson," Cole said in the same tone.

Merry's chin went up and she smirked. "Did you find what you were looking for in the stockyard?"

"Trent has a few bulls he's looking to buy. He wants to start his own herd." Cole shook his head. "I couldn't believe the price of the semen. It's ten thousand dollars for about a tenth of a teaspoon."

"Nice job if you can get it," Merry flirted.

It was like breathing with her, April thought. Cole, bless him, didn't seem to notice.

"You'd think after his accidents, he'd stay away from the bucking bulls," Merry said.

"You don't know Trent. It's in his blood. He doesn't ride anymore, but he's a hell of a coach."

"Is that what you do?"

"I help him with that and with teaching the kids how to rope and wrestle steer."

"I'm surprised Emily allows that," Merry said.

"It's not her school."

"It's her ranch."

Cole shrugged. "You, of all people, know the chances of the steer getting hurt is slim."

"I know. I'm just busting your balls. You ever miss getting out there?" She indicated the dusty arena.

"I miss the crowds and the excitement. I don't miss landing wrong on the ground."

Merry smiled, despite herself. "So April, is he as good as he says with rope?"

That was enough of that. "He's better with handcuffs," she said deadpanned.

"April Grayson," Merry scolded, genuinely shocked.

April laughed. It felt good to see Merry clutch her pearls for once. "Have a good ride. We'll go for drinks later."

Then, with another quick hug, April left her sister still gaping after them.

"Handcuffs?" Cole asked her in a low voice.

"I hope you don't mind, but I brought some toys for us to play with later." April patted his back when he choked.

"I don't mind at all. Who gets cuffed first?" he said, clearing his throat.

"We can take turns."

Cole grabbed her hand again. "I've got a game tonight."

"It's Vegas. Time is irrelevant."

"You're learning."

They made their way back to their seats after grabbing beers and some cheese fries to share. "Did you book the cruise yet?" she asked.

"Not yet," Cole said, licking cheese sauce off his fingers. "I couldn't figure out how to piggyback on your reservation, so I think I have to book my own cabin."

April frowned. "That's a waste of money. When we get back home on Monday, I'll call my travel agent and have her work her magic. The flights might be a little tricky, but the worst-case scenario is that we meet up at the airport or on the ship. But we can definitely stay in the same cabin."

"Okay, that works."

"Are you gambling with that money tonight?"

"I'm not planning on it. I put money away for the cruise and the bills I wanted to get rid of this month."

Relief sliced through her. "Great. I'm glad you did that. Now, you can enjoy yourself and have fun at the table." He was playing it safe for her. That was more romantic than a bouquet of flowers.

"Fun?" He cocked his head at her. "I guess it is fun. But this is a job, same as tossing hay bales around. When money doesn't matter, then it's just a game."

She nodded. "I guess I can see that. I get so disappointed when the slot machine eats all my quarters."

"But for a few minutes, you were entertained by the music, the lights, and the experience, right?"

"Right."

"So think of it as entertainment. You'd pay ten dollars for a book or a movie, right? For you, gambling is like that. For me, I'm betting that in six hours I can make a year's salary. And everything in me is focused on that goal. It's exhilarating and challenging, but it's not fun. If I want to have fun with cards, I'd play strip poker with you like I promised."

"I think I'm beginning to understand. You're different when you play. You're cold and intense."

"That's because you can't see my eyes."

"It's in your body language, too."

"All the players have a persona. I guess that's mine."

They watched the barrel racers swing around the barrels. April screamed herself hoarse for Merry when she took first place.

"Did you see how fast Raphael was?" April said, clinging to Cole. "I think he's even faster than Athena. But don't tell June I said so."

"I think Emily would give her left arm to ride that horse."

"He won't move like that unless Merry is riding him," April said, whistling and clapping as Merry waved to the crowd.

"Do you think Merry is having fun?"

April was going to say, 'of course,' but then she looked at her sister's face. She didn't see any joy at all. "A bit," she hedged. "But I think like you and poker, this has become a job instead of fun. It's sad."

"Why?"

"I remember how she and June used to look when they

were racing out of the chute—hair flying, smiling so wide their faces hurt, tightly controlling the horse, and then riding hell-bent for leather. But now, I think this has become commonplace for Merry. She was ready to move on to something new before this thing with June happened. I think we've seen one of her last rides."

"It's good to go out a winner," Cole said.

"Are you thinking of playing poker full-time?" she asked, wondering if they were on the brink of having a long-distance relationship.

"No, I've got to build up a bigger nest egg before I can try that again. I like working with the kids. And I like being in the same state as you. So aside from a big tournament here and there, the poker rooms in Las Vegas will be just a once-in-a-while thing."

She let out the breath she had been holding. "I'm glad. I like having you close to me."

Cole rubbed his thumb across her knuckles. "You've become very important to me. To be fair, I was hooked since our first night."

It would be hard for her to be in a serious relationship with a gambler, but it was a risk April was willing to take.

"Working with you so closely for the last month has made me realize I'm going to miss you when you're not there across the room from me," he added.

"I'll be out of the office by tax time, but I'll be there after work anytime you want me."

"Good." And the kiss he dropped on her lips was like a vow.

Chapter Twenty-Two

COLE SHOULDN'T HAVE checked his voicemail when they were on break. But he was having a hard time reading the table and needed a few minutes away from it to clear his head. Once the game started, it came out that he was playing against three Vegas poker dealers on their off-night. No matter what position he was in, he couldn't recreate the magic he had experienced in Texas. Not with these guys, anyway.

He should quit. He'd already lost everything he'd brought with him. April was here and they could still salvage the night with a rousing bought of sex with handcuffs and toys. It would take the sting out of the loss and, when they left tomorrow morning, at least he'd have a smile on his face. Cole could make the money back with the Texans the next time they were at Donovan's for poker night.

But then he saw that he had three missed messages. All from Gwen.

Shit.

He listened to the messages, having to sit down on the bench at the last one.

"Cole, your mother fell trying to go upstairs. We're taking

her to the hospital now. She hit her head. She's unconscious."

"Cole, I'm so sorry to tell you this over the phone, but your mom broke her hip in the fall. She's still unconscious."

"Cole your mother is in a coma. They think she had a stroke when she fell."

His eyes filled with tears and his throat closed. He had to get back home, but their flight was leaving in seven hours anyway. A few more hours wouldn't matter. What would matter was getting back the money that he lost. He swiped over to his banking app and transferred everything to his casino account. Should he start cold at another table or stay at the one he was at? Starting fresh after he had already invested a lot of time and money didn't appeal to him, but he knew that he was the weak link at the table he was sitting at.

"Ready to call it a night?" April said, sitting down next to him. She laid her head on his shoulder. It was easier to breathe when she was near.

"Not just yet," he said hoarsely.

He could feel her fighting not to say something. He didn't want to tell her about his mother. He wanted her to enjoy their last night in Las Vegas. He'd tell her on the plane tomorrow morning.

"Are you sure?" she said hesitantly.

"I'm sure," he said with more resolution than he felt.

"The handcuffs are waiting."

Her sweet cajoling voice coaxed a small smile from him. "Trust me, I wish I was free to take you up on your offer, but I've got a few more hours of work here."

She rolled her eyes, exasperated. "Fine. Merry has been trying to get me to zip-line down Fremont Street, but she's not going to wait much longer. Do you mind if I take her up on it?"

He was tempted to go just to watch her and her sister scream down five city blocks. "Only if you do it on your stomach, superhero style." Cole placed his arms out in front of him. "And get the video."

"Deal," she said, giving him a thumbs-up. And then she was sprinting off to catch her sister before Merry changed her mind about waiting for her. He watched her until she was out of sight. They hadn't had a lot of time to go on thrill rides or do any of the fun things in Vegas. Then again, he was working. First for Trent and now for himself. He'd thought he was finally over the hardships. But it seemed as if they were only just beginning.

Even though it was late, he tried to call Gwen, but it went to her voicemail. He left a message asking her to give him the name of the doctor who was treating his mother and any other information. His next call was to Jameson Hospital. They confirmed that his mother was there and stable for the time being. She was waiting for a room. The receptionist suggested he call back in the morning and by that time, they would know more about her condition. The woman also confirmed that his father was there with his mom, but he was sleeping while holding her hand. They had orderlies keeping an eye on both of them.

While she was explaining this to him, he searched for an earlier flight with no luck. "I can't be there any sooner than noon tomorrow," he said, trying to tamp down his frustration. He didn't want to take it out on her. She was being very helpful.

"Your home health care aide tried to get your father to go home, but he refused to leave your mom's side."

That sounded like his dad. Poor Gwen didn't have a chance of making him budge.

"She said she'll be back by seven a.m."

"I'll be on a plane by then," he said.

"Your mother's in good hands, Mr. Lockwood. We'll take care of her until you get here."

"Thank you."

He took a walk around the casino to clear his head. After a cup of coffee, he thought about going back to the room and getting a decent night's sleep. But he was too restless, and this was Vegas, after all. Desperate times called for desperate measures. Cole squared his shoulders and went off to find another poker game.

WHEN HER ALARM woke her up at the ungodly hour of five a.m., April regretted going to bed two hours ago. She regretted it even more when she realized there was no sign that Cole had come back to the hotel room last night. They had to check in for their flight in an hour. She wasn't too worried because they were less than two miles from the airport and the shuttle was reserved to pick them up at five thirty. But after a quick shower, he still wasn't back. She called his cell phone.

"Where are you?" she asked.

"I'll meet you at McCarran at the gate."

"You are not still on the gambling floor," she said, exasperated.

"April, please. I'll explain when I see you. Can you just throw my stuff in my carry-on?"

"We have to check in by six," she said.

"I know. I've got my ticket on my phone. I'll be there. I promise."

"Unbelievable," she said to the dead phone.

Getting dressed, she grumbled to herself. It was ridiculous to stay out all night when you had an early flight. Even Wild April had been in bed by three. She knew she should have gone back out when he wasn't in the room waiting for her. But he hadn't answered his phone and she didn't even know which casino he had ended up in. Luckily, he had packed light and both their luggage were rollers. After a quick look around the room, she left a tip for the maid and checked out via the television.

April half-expected Cole to make it to the shuttle, but he didn't. Nor was he there when she checked in for the flight, or even for the mind-numbing wait to get through security. She grabbed a quick breakfast sandwich and a canned coffee drink and stuffed them into her bag while she waited at the gate. She rang him several times, but the calls immediately went to voicemail. Either his battery had run down or he'd turned off his phone. In any event, when they started boarding, she left him a final message:

"The plane is leaving and I'm on it. You have a gambling problem. Don't call me. I need some time to cool down. I'll see you at work tomorrow morning."

Shades of her mother's boyfriends haunted her. She didn't want to think that Cole had done something stupid, but she knew in her gut that he had. April wanted to throw her phone down and stomp on it in frustration, but that would only inconvenience her.

Cole had asked her along on this weekend as a date. At least they'd had a good time Friday night after the stockyard show. They had gone to dinner and a show, but the long day had caught up to them and they turned in early after leisurely making love to make up for the frenzied plane sex that morning. Then Saturday had been a whirlwind. She still couldn't believe he'd played poker all night.

Yes, she could. What she couldn't believe was that he'd left her to check out of the hotel and fly home all alone.

April peered out the airplane window, hoping Cole would make it at the last minute. But when the plane taxied down the runway, she eased the seat back and put on her sleep mask. Maybe she'd feel better after her nap. Only when they landed at Austin International, the anger she'd felt toward him had changed to hurt.

Chapter Twenty-Three

C OLE KNEW HE was walking into a fight Monday morning. He considered taking the coward's way out and calling in sick, but he knew prolonging this discussion would just make it worse. His mother had come out of her coma late last night, but she was looking at a long road to recovery. The swelling in her brain tissue had lessened and she was still groggy and weak. His father had finally agreed to go home with Gwen to get some sleep on the condition that Cole stayed with his mother. He had been glad to do it. It gave him some time to think and plan.

Unfortunately, it hadn't taken him very long to realize that he was fucked. He had lost everything. The sixty thousand and the money for the cruise. If there was a high-stakes game next month at Donovan's, he didn't even have the buy-in. He didn't know when he'd ever get the buy-in again. And now there were more medical bills.

Reluctantly, he trudged down the stairs. His father and Gwen had come back this morning and he showered and took a quick catnap. He was defeated and exhausted, but he tried not to let it show. He had to brace himself for April's anger and take it. He deserved it. He had tried everything to come back from the loss. Well, almost everything. He hadn't accepted the casino's offer of a line of credit. That way led to madness. But he had abandoned April at the airport, and he was sorry.

She was already at her desk, typing away. His carry-on bag was by his chair.

"Hey," he said.

April looked up and then ran into his arms, hugging him tightly.

"What's this?" he asked, closing his eyes. He needed the hug, and he hugged her back for a long time.

"Trent told me about your mother."

Figured. He had called Trent on Sunday, before Cole's mother woke up, to let him know that depending on what happened, he might have to take some time off.

"I'm so sorry," she said, squeezing him. "Is there anything I can do?"

"You're doing it," he said, sadly. He didn't deserve her comfort and he forced himself to step away. "It's me who should be apologizing. I'm so sorry for abandoning you in Las Vegas. I was at a table trying to at least win some of my money back."

She held up a hand. "We can talk about that later. I can see you're at wit's end. Why don't you go back upstairs and get some sleep? Billy said he could cover your classes."

"No. I'm here and the kids need me. Billy can be too impatient with the slow learners."

Caressing his cheek, April said, "You're a good man."

He barked out a half laugh. "Am I? It sure doesn't feel

like it." Cole turned away from her. This hurt like a bitch. She deserved a man who would be free to be wild and crazy with her. One who wasn't buried under bills. He couldn't be an anchor around her neck. "I lost it all. And then I went into my account and took out more. I drained my account and I lost that too."

She inhaled sharply, but didn't say anything.

He wished she would yell at him or say that she told him so.

"I can help," April said instead.

Wincing, his fingers clenched into fists. That was worse. He was expecting her anger. He didn't need her pity. And he wouldn't accept any money from her. Whirling back around, he growled out, "I don't need your help."

The sadness in her eyes almost undid him.

"I spent all morning on this," she said. "Just listen to me. Sell the house. Move them into a ground-floor apartment with an assisted living program. Use the money to pay off the medical debts as much as you can, while leaving them a monthly stipend. I have it all worked out." She tried to hand him a notebook.

"It's not my decision to sell the house. And my father is in no shape to talk about it right now."

"Of course," she said. "But when things calm down, I think he'll see that these apartments are really the best of both worlds. They can have their autonomy, but be safe and protected, too."

Cole didn't think his father would go for it, but he didn't have the heart to disappoint her. Not when she had worked so hard for him. He took the notebook. "I'll see what he says. But for right now, I'm going to have to go back to working nights and weekends."

April squeezed his arm. "Give it a few weeks."

He pulled away. "I think you missed the part where I told you I'm broke. I'm going to be living paycheck to paycheck for a while. I'm not proud of what I did. I know better, but I just thought…" Cole looked at the ceiling. "I thought that this time it would be different."

"Cole, I grew up in a trailer. I know how to stretch a dollar. Hell, I've got a degree in it. Let me help you."

"I've got to do this myself," he said.

"No, you don't. That's what I'm here for."

"April, you spent your entire life looking after your mother and sisters. Now that you're finally coming into your own, I will be damned if I drag you down by taking care of me."

"What are you saying?" she said, swallowing hard.

"I'm saying I don't deserve you. You deserve someone who has their shit together and for a moment, I thought that guy was me."

"It is you," she whispered.

Cole ran his hand over his face. "Not yet it's not."

"I'll wait," she said.

"I can't let you do that."

"You're not letting me do anything!" April shouted. "I want to do this."

He loved her. He loved her too much to let her settle for him. "April, as soon as I save enough money, I'm entering another high-stakes game."

Her mouth dropped open in shock and she gawked at him. "Are you out of your mind?" she said finally.

"This time I'll quit when I'm ahead," he said.

She gave a half laugh and the disappointment in her eyes almost drove him to his knees. "No, you won't," she said.

Taking a deep breath, Cole said, "I think you should move your office to the ranch house until you're done with Trent's taxes. It will be less of a distraction."

She closed her eyes and sighed. "Don't do this."

He couldn't resist taking her face in his hands and kissing her forehead. "You're better off without me."

"Don't you think I should be the one to decide that?"

"Please don't make this harder than it already is. I need to concentrate on my parents and keeping the bills paid."

"If this is what you need, then fine," she said, reluctantly.

"It's for the best." Then he turned around and left before she could change his mind.

APRIL HAD JUST carried in the first file box from her car to the sunroom in the ranch house when Emily came downstairs.

"What's going on?" she said.

"My desk has been moved to your sunroom. Trent said it was okay. I hope I'm not intruding."

"No, not at all. Kelly and my mom will be glad for the company. Why are you moving from the school?"

"Drama," April said. "I guess this is why office romances are frowned upon."

"What happened in Vegas?"

April laughed. "I can't tell you. It's against the law. What happens in Vegas stays in Vegas, don't you know? Suffice it to say, whoever says money doesn't buy happiness doesn't realize it's easier to cry in a Mercedes than in a cardboard box."

Emily followed her outside to help with the boxes. "I hear you about money problems. Last year killed any progress we'd made on the ranch's bills."

April winced. "It was hard on everybody."

"And now that Cole's mom is back in the hospital, I'm sure he's worried sick."

"He is," April said. "And he's not thinking too clearly right now. I'm trying to cut him slack, but he's so damned stubborn."

"I'm marrying stubborn," Emily said. "Donovan wanted to put off the wedding until next year, but I didn't want to wait. I offered to go to the courthouse and have the justice of the peace marry us, but you would have thought I'd offered to bring rattlesnakes in the house with the reaction I got."

"Your mama wants a big wedding?"

"To be honest, so do I, but it seems so frivolous when there are bills to pay."

April had a twinge of guilt about going on her cruise. She had already paid for most of it, but she supposed she could get a refund. Even if she did, there was no way that Cole would accept the money if she offered him a loan. Or would he? She paused in the doorway, letting Emily go in first. What if she told him she had stake money for his next poker game?

Groaning, she shook her head. She was as bad as he was. Except, she believed in him. And he wasn't going to stop playing. If she offered him a stake, he could get back in the local poker games. And that would at least mean that he wouldn't have to kill himself working two jobs. As much as she wanted to go on her cruise, she had waited this long. It would be more fun if she could go with Cole anyway. She wasn't sure how she would explain it to her sisters, though. They would accuse her of acting like Mama and giving away her hard-earned money for some pretty face. But this was different. Sighing, she walked in the house and set the box down. At least, she thought it was.

As she went out for another, she saw Emily with her hands on her hips talking with the man from the Bluebonnet Country Club. That must have been why he had looked so familiar. April must have seen him around. She tried not to listen in, but Emily was loud by nature.

"Charlie, you know better than to hang out around the house. Donovan would lose his shit."

"I just wanted to check on things. There seems to be a lot of activity going on here."

April walked closer, just in case Emily needed some help.

"Ma'am," Charlie said, dipping his hat.

"You're a poker player, right?" April said. "I saw you at the country club the other night."

"Poker?" Emily said.

Charlie winced.

"I'm pretty sure that's a parole violation."

"I'd appreciate if you kept that between the three of us," he said.

"It's your life," Emily said. "But if you want Donovan to come around, it would help if you didn't slip back into your old ways."

"Poker is perfectly legal."

"Uh-huh." Emily shook her head. "I've got to get some work done once I settle April in the sunroom. Stop skulking around here and go back to the retreat."

"I'm not a bad man, Emily."

Her face softened. "The man I love says differently. But I'll keep an open mind."

"I appreciate that."

Charlie winked at April and walked back toward the retreat center.

"How long do you think he was standing there?" April said.

"With Charlie, who knows? He's harmless, but sneaky." They went in the house and set the boxes on the wide glass table.

"Who is he?"

"He's Donovan's father. He's also an ex-con who runs a bunch of rehab retreats for white-collar criminals at Janice's center," Emily said.

"Oh right, Kelly mentioned that. She said he and Donovan weren't exactly on speaking terms." April set up her computer. "He seems nice, though."

"He's very charming," Emily said. "I haven't figured out yet if he's full of shit or not. He wants to rebuild his relationship with his son, but I'm not going to let him hurt Donovan again. Charlie has been on his best behavior, but I don't really trust him." Dusting off her hands, Emily shuddered at the paperwork. "I don't envy you this job."

"It's not so bad. I'm almost done."

"Maybe I should have you look at the ranch's books."

April didn't know whether to be happy to have a new client or worried that Emily couldn't really afford her. "I do free consultations," she said. "I'd be happy to look, but you're cutting it close to the tax deadline."

Emily looked lost in thought. "I'll let you know. I'll see you later. I've got some things to take care of outside in the fresh air."

"Enjoy," April said. She didn't start work right away, though. Instead, she opened her email and read the terms of her agreement with the cruise company. It would bother her all day wondering if there was a penalty if she canceled this far in advance.

Chapter Twenty-Four

I T HAD ONLY been a week, but Cole missed April desperately. He swore that his office still smelled like her light perfume. The room felt empty without her sitting across from him, nibbling on a pencil and shuffling papers.

When he came back from teaching roping to his middle-school class, he was surprised to see Charlie Lincoln sitting at April's abandoned desk with his feet crossed at the ankles on the desk's top.

"Can I help you?"

"Your friend Vic never called."

"Donovan said you're bad news."

"Donovan's biased." Charlie set his boots on the ground. "There's another game in two weeks."

Damn. Cole shook his head. "I'm not going to be in it."

"Are you nuts? It's easy money."

"I don't have the buy-in. Besides, I have to work." Cole was so damned tired though, he was ready to drop. He caught little catnaps when he could. Mostly when he was visiting his mother or on his lunch and dinner breaks. He was bone-weary and heartsick.

"I'll stake you."

Cole stiffened. "I don't want to be involved in anything illegal."

"Me neither. And I've got more to lose than you do, believe me."

"What's the split?" he asked before he could stop himself.

"Nothing. You keep it all."

Snorting, Cole flung himself into his desk chair. "Are you Santa Claus, handing out ten grand like it was nothing?"

"I didn't say I didn't want anything in return."

"If it's not illegal, then you have my attention." At the very least, it would be a good story to tell April. His heart sunk. Oh right, he was staying away from her for her own good.

"I've made some mistakes in my past. Bad ones. I paid for my crimes and I'm out on parole."

Cole nodded.

"My son, Donovan, hasn't forgiven me, though. And maybe I don't deserve his forgiveness. But I want it."

Cole could relate. "Everyone makes mistakes. Not everyone has the balls to admit it. Maybe Donovan will come around once he realizes you've changed. You have changed, right?"

"I am not the same man I was twenty years ago. But I can't wait for him to see that. So here's what I propose. I'll give you one hundred thousand dollars."

Gripping the arms of his chair, Cole stared at him in disbelief.

"You take half of it for yourself. The other half, you take to Emily and tell her that you want to invest it in the ranch.

I will be your silent partner for that half of the money and whatever dividends or not come from that investment, I keep."

"You can't invest in the ranch yourself?"

"I can't even get my son to have a cup of coffee with me and Emily won't take my money."

"Is it dirty money?"

Charlie barked out a laugh. "No, it's actually Donovan's mother's money. She had a nest egg that we never touched. She would have wanted to help her son. She's gone now."

"I'm sorry," he said, thinking of his own mother.

"That's it. I don't need a contract. Just a handshake."

"That's awfully trusting of you."

"I know how to read people."

"Are you sure that the Sullivans are even looking for investors?"

"I have it on good authority that they need this money. They trust you. You can tell them that the money came from poker winnings. Tell them anything you want...as long as you don't tell them it came from me." Charlie stood up and held out his hand. "Do we have a deal?"

Cole stood up. "Maybe. What if I don't want to use my half to play poker with?"

"Honestly, I don't give a damn what you do with it. But I've seen you play, and you've got a gift, kid. You can double that easy at the game."

"Or I could lose it all," he said, thinking of April.

"Something's spooked you."

Shaking himself out of it, Cole shook Charlie's hand.

He'd be an idiot not to take this deal. He could help out the Sullivans and maybe solve some problems at the same time. There was a time to take risks and a time to play it safe.

"I'm not going to let you hurt them," Cole said, tightening his grip on Charlie's hand.

"It's the furthest thing in my mind." Charlie's eyes went flint gray, but Cole held on until he was sure Charlie knew he meant business.

"Then we have a deal."

"I'll have the cash to you by tonight."

"One hundred thousand dollars in cash?" Cole choked.

"You think you're the only one who has a fixer for underground poker games?" Charlie glanced away with a grim look on his face. "Those kind of tables you don't want any part of, though. Stick with Vic." Then Charlie shook off his mood and smiled jovially at him again. "Give them the money as soon as you can." Charlie walked to the door. "And remember, this conversation never happened, and I was never here."

"That's a little overdramatic, don't you think?"

Charlie saluted him with two fingers and left.

Taking out his phone, Cole called his father. This wasn't going to be an easy conversation, but it was time to consider other options. Options that April had suggested. He flipped through her notebook and felt a surge of hope. "Dad, we need to talk."

APRIL HAD JUST finished with Athena when she saw Cole leaning up against his truck, waiting for her. It hurt seeing him and not knowing if a kiss and hug would be welcome. She took her time putting the tools away and washing up. When she couldn't procrastinate anymore, she approached him.

"You look rested," she said.

"At peace," he replied and held out his hand. She took it gratefully and let him pull her into his arms for a long kiss that she never wanted to end. She felt tears prick and she clung to him. He didn't let go, just kept kissing her.

"All right, get a room," Janice said. "I'm closing up the barn, so you don't have to go home, but you can't stay here."

"What do you say?" Cole asked. "Will you come home with me?"

April nodded. "I'll follow you in my car." Because she didn't trust herself not to have truck sex with him. It had been a long week without him. There was only another week's work before she was done with Trent's taxes. Luckily, she had several clients lined up, but the thought of not being close to Cole left her feeling like she had a hole in her heart.

She parked next to his truck, then took his hand and let him lead her up to his apartment.

"I missed you so damn much," he said, closing the door behind them.

"I've been here all week, dummy."

"I am a dummy. Forgive me?"

"Hell yes." She began to strip.

"Wait," he said, weakly. "I need to tell you a few things."

"Tell me afterward," April said flinging her bra off and working on her pants.

Cole just stood there with his jaw hanging open.

"I should have taken you home and showed you my new pole dance routine, but I was afraid you'd change your mind." Naked, she knelt on his bed and crooked her finger.

"Damn, I can't resist you." He sat on the bed next to her.

"Let me help you out of those clothes," she said, and eagerly began divesting him of his shirt. She purred in satisfaction when he caressed her body and kissed her. When they were both naked, she took his cock in her hand and stroked it.

"Is that what you want?" He lifted his mouth from hers.

"I want it all. I never want to spend another week like this one. I don't care what happens. I want to be with you."

"Good," he said. "I want that too. April, I love you."

His words shuddered through her and she wrapped her arms around him and took him down to the bed with her. "I love you too, you idiot. Now, make love to me."

Hooking her legs around his waist, she wiggled until she felt his hardness pulsing hot near her opening. Cole teased her, moving along the edges. She held on to his shoulder and writhed until he slipped into her wetness.

"Finally," she groaned.

"I'm not wearing a condom." He panted, holding himself still.

She was having none of that. "It's okay. I haven't been with anyone but you in a long time, and I started taking the pill as soon as we had sex the second time."

"I'm clean, too," he gritted out.

"Then take me fast because I love the feel of you inside me."

April's toes curled when he bucked into her hard enough to slam the headboard back against the wall. The creak of the mattress springs added to the noise of their bodies slapping together in an erotic song and dance.

"I needed this," she moaned.

His hard length slid in and out in a punishing rhythm that she lost herself to.

"I want you."

"You have me," he grunted. The muscles in his arms corded with his effort and she sighed, melting into his onslaught.

Her hips rose and met him stroke for stroke in a passionate race to climax. When his teeth grazed the sweet spot on her neck, she lost the fight and trembled. "Cole," she gasped, staring at the ceiling as a shockwave of pleasure tumbled over her.

His roar of triumph followed as he emptied himself inside her.

Her legs felt rubbery and boneless. "I can't move," she said.

"Mmm," he said, rolling on his back and taking her with him. They kissed while Cole rubbed his hands up and down her sides. When it became sticky and uncomfortable, he carried her into the shower. "Let's get you nice and clean," he said, then fingered her to another orgasm while she clung to him.

"I love you," she said as she came.

He held her until the shockwaves passed.

"My turn," April said, grabbing his cock in a soapy grip. She rubbed him until he came in her hand, moaning his pleasure into her mouth.

"I love you, too."

Satiated for now, she finished up in the shower and let him dry her off with a fluffy towel.

They went back to bed and got under the covers this time.

"So what did you want to talk to me about?" she said when he leaned up on his elbow to look down at her.

"I wanted to let you know that you were right and I was wrong."

She cupped his face in her hands. "There isn't a right and wrong."

"My dad agreed to sell the house. We're putting it on the market next week. When my mom leaves rehab, hopefully she'll get a few weeks to say goodbye to it. We're looking for a ground-level apartment with assisted living like you suggested. Gwen had a few ideas."

April kissed him hard on the mouth. "I'm so proud of you. That couldn't have been easy."

"It wasn't and I suspect that it will get worse before it gets better, but I wouldn't have even considered it if it hadn't been for you."

"I'm so happy for you. Does that mean you're not going to work nights and weekends anymore?"

"It does," he said. "There's more, though."

"Okay." She curled up against him.

"I've recently come into some money."

"How?" April narrowed her eyes.

"This remains between you and me, but I went into business with Charlie Lincoln."

"Donovan's father?"

"There's some bad blood between the two of them. But he wants the Three Sisters Ranch to succeed so he gave me fifty thousand dollars to invest in it. Emily was happy to sign me on as an investor. Charlie is a silent partner. They can't know the money came from him."

She rubbed his arm. "That's fantastic, I think. What did he need you for?"

"He said Donovan wouldn't accept the money if it came from him. But that's not all."

"Oh."

"Charlie is going to take one hundred percent of the dividends from the ranch investment I'm making on his behalf."

"Well, that seems fair. It is his money and he's probably going to have to wait a while to see a return on his investment."

"He paid me fifty thousand to be his silent partner and to keep my mouth shut."

"Where does a man like that get one hundred thousand dollars?" April said, wondering if Charlie Lincoln was doing something he shouldn't be.

"He says it's Donovan's late mother's money, but he also said he's been playing poker in underground games, so who knows?"

"What did you do with the money?" she whispered.

"I paid down a bunch of bills, and then I booked the cabin next to yours on the cruise."

"Cole, I was going to try and get a refund. Thank goodness we talked before I did. It would've been like the *Gift of the Magi* only with drink coupons."

"What are you talking about? This cruise is what you have been dreaming about all your life."

"Actually, I've been dreaming about you all my life. And once I had you, I didn't want to let you go. I was going to get a refund and give you the money so you could play poker and build your cash flow back up."

Cole froze. "You were going to stake me?"

"Yes, I believe in you. I know you could do it. You just hit a bad table in Vegas."

"Several of them," he said dryly.

"Maybe you need to stick to Texas then." She laid her head on his arm. "Are you sure you want to use the money for the cruise? It seems wasteful when your parents need it more."

"My parents are going to be fine. Trent has already agreed to let me take the month off next year. I've worked hard for this. I want to do this for me. And for us."

"I'm so lucky to have you," April said.

"I'm the lucky one. You would have stayed with me, even though I was riddled with debt and working too many hours to spend any time with you."

"Of course, I would. Things would have gotten better.

Even if Charlie Lincoln hadn't come along." She frowned. "Are you sure he's on the up and up?"

"I think he wants a relationship with his son. I think he likes the Three Sisters Ranch and wants to help. And if there's one thing I learned by being with you, it's that people can change if they want to, my wild Grayson sister."

"Yeah, but deep down I'm still boring April."

"And deep down, maybe Charlie is still a grifter, but I think he means well. Will you keep our secret?"

She nodded. "I will unless it looks like someone is in danger or can be hurt from the secret."

"Fair enough," Cole said. "Then I have another question for you."

"Anything."

"Marry me. Let's make that cruise our honeymoon."

April sat up. "Are you serious? We haven't known each other that long."

"That's not something a wild Grayson would say."

"You're right," she said, shaking her head.

But he just smiled. Then, reaching into the bedside table, he pulled out a ring box. "April Grayson, will you marry me?"

Her hands were shaking when she opened it. The band of diamonds was twisted like a rodeo rope and on top was a bright red ruby.

"A wild ring for my wild love." Cole slipped it on her finger.

"Of course, I'll marry you." She kissed him until the flames of desire tickled both of them.

"I can't promise you that it will be easy, but I will love you with all my heart, through the good times and the bad. We both know I'm still going to take some bone-headed risks."

"And I'm going to overthink and over-plan for things."

"But we'll be in this together. I'll lead you into temptation every chance I get, and you can be my voice of reason."

"We'll meet in the middle," April said, sinking back into the bed. And with Cole, that was the only place she ever wanted to be.

The End

Want more? Check out Janice and Nate's story in
The Cowboy's Heart!

Join Tule Publishing's newsletter for more great reads and weekly deals!

If you enjoyed *A Cowboy for April*,
you'll love the other books in the...

Three Sisters Ranch series

Book 1: *The Cowboy's Daughter*

Book 2: *The Cowboy's Hunt*

Book 3: *The Cowboy's Heart*

Book 4: *A Cowboy for April*
View the series here!

Book 5: *A Cowboy for June*
Coming September 2021!

Book 6: *A Cowboy for Merry*
Coming November 2021!

Available now at your favorite online retailer!

About the Author

USA Today bestselling author, Jamie K. Schmidt, writes erotic contemporary love stories and paranormal romances. Her steamy, romantic comedy, Life's a Beach, reached #65 on USA Today, #2 on Barnes & Noble and #9 on Amazon and iBooks. Her Club Inferno series from Random House's Loveswept line has hit both the Amazon and Barnes & Noble top one hundred lists. The first book in the series, Heat, put her on the USA Today bestseller list for the first time, and is a #1 Amazon bestseller. Her book Stud is a 2018 Romance Writers of America Rita® Finalist in Erotica. Her dragon paranormal romance series has been called "fun and quirky" and "endearing." Partnered with New York Times bestselling author and former porn actress, Jenna Jameson, Jamie's hardcover debut, SPICE, continues Jenna's FATE trilogy.

Visit her website at jamiekschmidt.weebly.com.